Praise for *Tell Me I'm Worthless*

"A gripping, hallucinogenic haunted house novel as righteously angry as it is horrifying, *Tell Me I'm Worthless* unflinchingly lays bare the personal and cultural scars we wear, endure, and inflict."   **—Paul Tremblay, author of *The Pallbearers Club***

"An utterly harrowing experience. Like all iconic masterworks of horror fiction, *Tell Me I'm Worthless* rips you apart and then tenderly pieces you together until you're something entirely new."   **—Eric LaRocca, author of *Things Have Gotten Worse Since We Last Spoke***

"Chilling, bone-deep horror as humane as it is hideous."
—Gretchen Felker-Martin, author of *Manhunt*

"A defiant love letter to the lost, reminding us that win or lose, live or die, we can still save our souls by choosing love."
—Maya Deane, author of *Wrath Goddess Sing*

"Punk in every sense of the word."
—Eliza Clark, author of *Boy Parts*

"Gripping, unsettling, compulsive, spicy, and, in the end, deeply moving."   **—Molly Smith, coauthor of *Revolting Prostitutes***

"An important book, as transgressive and trans as they come."
—Isabel Waidner, author of *Sterling Karat Gold*

"A sharp and visceral novel which bends the horror genre to its will."
—Julia Armfield, author of *Our Wives Under the Sea*

T0036041

TELL ME I'M WORTHLESS

ALISON RUMFITT

NIGHTFIRE

TOR PUBLISHING GROUP

NEW YORK

TELL ME I'M WORTHLESS

Copyright © 2021 by Alison Rumfitt

A Nightfire Book
Published by Tom Doherty Associates/Tor Publishing Group
120 Broadway
New York, NY 10271

tornightfire.com

Nightfire™ is a trademark of Macmillan Publishing Group, LLC.

Library of Congress Cataloging-in-Publication Data

Names: Rumfitt, Alison, author.
Title: Tell me I'm worthless / Alison Rumfitt.
Other titles: Tell me I am worthless
Description: First U.S. edition. | New York : Nightfire/Tom Doherty
    Associates, 2023.
Identifiers: LCCN 2022032718 (print) | LCCN 2022032719 (ebook) |
    ISBN 9781250866233 (trade paperback) | ISBN 9781250866240 (ebook)
Subjects: LCGFT: Horror fiction. | Fiction.
Classification: LCC PR6118.U74 T45 2023 (print) | LCC PR6118.U74
    (ebook) | DDC 823/.92—dc23/eng/20220708
LC record available at https://lccn.loc.gov/2022032718
LC ebook record available at https://lccn.loc.gov/2022032719

Our books may be purchased in bulk for promotional, educational, or business use. Please contact your local bookseller or the Macmillan Corporate
and Premium Sales Department at 1-800-221-7945, extension 5442, or by
email at MacmillanSpecialMarkets@macmillan.com.

Originally published in 2021 by Cipher Press, 105 Ink Court,
419 Wick Lane, London, E3 2PX, United Kingdom

First U.S. Edition: 2023

Printed in the United States of America

0 9 8 7 6 5

SORRY FOR LETTING YOU HAUNT THIS BOOK

Tell Me I'm Worthless is a book about two things, primarily, and those things are trauma and fascism. I thought it important to include a content warning here, at the start, to say that. In dealing with those topics, the novel covers racism, antisemitism, transphobia, rape (both in abstract and graphic ways), self-harm and suicide.

You might disagree with the inclusion of a content warning at the start of a book. If that is the case, then you are within your rights to do so. Please do not, however, complain to my publisher about this. The choice was mine, and mine alone.

Fascism, like desire, is scattered everywhere, in separate bits and pieces, within the whole social realm; it crystallizes in one place or another, depending on the relationships of force. It can be said of fascism that it is all-powerful and, at the same time, ridiculously weak. And whether it is the former or the latter depends on the capacity of collective arrangements, subject-groups, to connect the social libido, on every level, with the whole range of revolutionary machines of desire.

Félix Guattari, "Everybody Wants to be a Fascist,"
Semio-text(e), Vol. II, No. 3

But how often—really—do you think about the grand strategy of gender? The mess of history and sociology, biology and game theory that gave rise to your pants and your hair and your salary? The *casus belli*?

Often, you might say. All the time. It haunts me.

Then you, more than anyone, helped make me.

Isabel Fall, "Helicopter Story," *Clarkesworld Magazine*, Issue 160

PROLOGUE

THE FACE IN THE WALL

Long after the House is gone, it's there.

The boy and his parents moved into the new flat around a year ago. It was a new flat, but it didn't feel new, it was damp, and cold, and it had felt hostile to them the moment they hauled their stuff inside. The boy's mother knew, in that moment, that they had made a terrible mistake, but by that point it was too late. They lived here. They could not afford to live somewhere else.

The boy's mother and father have been worrying. His grades have never been anything special, but now they seem to have slipped even further downward. He doesn't have any friends, and, even worse, he is utterly uninterested in making any. When they ask him if he wants to join any after-school clubs or sports teams, he just shrugs. They wonder if he's autistic, but his dad scoffs at the idea. His dad is the kind of man who thinks having an autistic son would mean there was something wrong with him. His dad, a big man with a red face, sits on the sofa in front of the TV ranting loudly about how *fucking immigrants* are keeping him from finding work. The boy can hear this, through his bedroom door. He spends a lot of time in his bedroom. It's small and dark. His mum tried to get him to put up some posters, but to put up posters you have to like things and he isn't sure he likes anything. He knows that there are things he should like – football, rappers, action movies. Boys like things like that. But he cannot bring himself to feel anything towards them beyond a mild, passing curiosity.

In his bedroom, the light hanging from the ceiling flickers, the bulb threatening to burst. Damp creeps through the wallpaper above his bed. He looks at the damp stain sometimes and thinks that he sees shapes in it. Eyes, a wide gaping mouth, opening up to swallow him whole. He is twelve now and thinks he should be over seeing monsters in his wallpaper, but even so, he asks his mum to try and sort it out. She gets his dad to re-paper the room, and for some time it works, the stains, and the shapes that hide within the stains, are gone. But two months later they are back, and, although it doesn't seem possible, larger than they had been. He can still see the shapes. He can still see the damp forming wide white eyes, and a twisted screaming mouth, and in that mouth the impression of a tongue and of teeth. It keeps him up at night. In his dreams, the shape becomes clearer, becomes a woman, and the screaming woman, her limbs all bent at strange angles around her, pushes out through the brick, through the paper, tearing it away to reach out into his bedroom and grab him. When she grabs him, he wakes up crying. At first, his mum comes into his room and hugs him until he goes back to sleep. After a while, she gives up. I mean, what's the use. He does this most nights. His dad says maybe she coddles him too much, if she keeps hugging him until he stops crying then he'll be a poof and he won't have a fucking poof for a son.

The boy begins to Google some of the things that his dad says, on the old computer which he has at his desk. He was given it for school, but he barely uses it for school. Instead he mostly uses it to search for those phrases his dad repeats under his breath when he drinks too much. My dad's right, he thinks. About these things. About the immigrants and the gays and the feminists and BLM tearing down statues, *historic* statues, iconic parts of our heritage, and actually his dad doesn't go far enough... The boy discovers forums where other people, older boys and men, mostly, tell him about the way the world really is: a vast conspiracy, of mass immigration, of Jews in the media, of feminists, of ahistorical cultural Marxism telling lies about the past. Manipulating the youth. They're in the schools. In his school, too. They're diversity hires, they're teachers asking for pupils' pronouns. Sometimes, one of the older men asks him for pictures of himself. It seems wrong, but he sends them, anyway, pictures of him naked in the grainy camera of his webcam, sent to anonymous accounts.

Mostly, though, they all want to stay hidden. They write out strings of slurs. They say they are going to do something. Something's coming, they tell the boy. Get ready for the storm, and make sure you're on the right side. The boy thinks, well, I have to make sure I'm on the right side. I have to do something. The face in the wall twists further, the mouth gets wider, the eyes get more frantic. But he doesn't have nightmares about it anymore. He doesn't wake up at night screaming. His mum and his dad are happy about that, at least. Maybe their strange little boy is going to be okay. They did a good job with him, right? They're doing a good job with him. Given the circumstances. Given the lack of money, and the shitty flat. And the government, and the state of the world. And the way things seem to be going. They did a good job, they tell themselves, we did a good job, we're raising a good kid, we've brought up a good son, over and over and over, insisting this to themselves and to anyone who will listen, repeating it until it makes them sick.

PART 1

THE DECLINE OF WESTERN WOMANHOOD

ALICE

It makes you sick.

This room, it makes you sick. It makes *me* sick. It's all angular and wrong, and the angles join in conversation with each other. They become hateful. They begin to tell you that they hate you and that they want you to die, somehow, that maybe they'll be the ones to kill you, or maybe they will convince you to kill yourself, with words, economic manipulation, gentrification, every weapon at their disposal. Because you didn't deserve to live, at least not *here*, in this room, in this building, in this part of the city. You should go somewhere else. You make us sick, the angles and the walls say, you'd be better off far from here, or dead, or both.

I hate living here. The rent is okay, I suppose, but the heating doesn't reach the top floor, where I am. On cold days I can see my breath in the air. And the inside of the windows fills with condensation, the corners of the room with creeping mould. I emailed the landlord about this, during winter, with my duvet wrapped close around me, and he responded telling me I needed to air the flat out by opening up the windows. But that's not really why I hate living here. This flat, and my bedroom in particular, reminds me of another place, another room in another part of the city. It doesn't look much like that place. It looks like a normal flat. Messy. Too messy. It's not really in how the place looks, but it feels the same, I can feel the air pressing in all around me, eyes watching me. Maybe that's why I moved in. This flat doesn't hate me, not really. Its hate is only a pale imitation of real, true hate. This room is not passionate. It still hates, but it only hates because, well, what else is it going to do. How else is it supposed to feel about me? Rooms sit and stew. They take in the things you do in them. Their walls soak up every action you take between them, and those actions become part of the bricks and the plaster. Maybe I made it hate me. I can be hateful, to myself and to others. I try not to be. I try to be better. I have to believe that everything I do has a destination to it, that everything I do means I have control, over my environment, my relationships, my life. My job, if I had one.

I move flats a lot. I don't feel comfortable staying in the same place for long, and in every house or flat that I've been in for the past five years, there has been a room where the house or the flat is concentrated to an absurd degree. In that room, the air grows thick and the spirit of the building becomes near-physical. The less rooms you have in your flat, the more concentrated this is. The less income you generate, the less rooms you can have in your flat, the thicker the air, the more hateful the atmosphere. I don't know if this is how it really works but it is what I tell myself.

I don't have many friends, but last year I began to ask whoever I could about hauntings, in the vague hope that somebody would understand what I meant when I said 'hauntings'. Most people have a ghost story of some kind, even if they don't believe in ghosts. Maybe their Great-grandma came to sit at the end of their bed for a month after she died, or they heard footsteps from the attic where there couldn't have been anyone to make them. I'd try to ask casually, at bars or on the internet, *have you ever experienced a haunting?* I made sure to phrase it like that. Not *have you ever seen a ghost?* I wanted to know about hauntings, specifically. One common thread which interested me was that many of the people who answered said that their places of work were haunted. This was actually more common than peoples' houses being haunted, which I thought was strange, but then again, Bly Manor from *The Turn of the Screw* was a place of work for the Governess and every big imposing house in the country has people working in it, cleaning, cooking and these days, now nobody lives in them, giving tours, maybe acting out scenes for tourists.

One girl told me that she worked as a cleaner for some offices which were housed in this absurdly tall old townhouse. She had to clean a few of the rooms, kitchens, toilets, but mostly the stairs, which wound up and up in sharp lines like a tower. But, after a couple of shifts, something strange started to happen. When she cleaned the lower landings and stairs, she could hear somebody doing the same above her. Moving about. Opening and closing doors. Vacuuming the floors.

She could hear their footsteps on the hard wood of the steps, echoing down from above. She thought this was strange – she had been told she would be working alone, and the sheet in the downstairs reception had said that everybody who worked here had signed out. When she ascended the stairs to work on the offices up there, and see who it was that was cleaning, everything was deserted, and still dirty. She stopped and listened then, and heard somebody below, cleaning the floors that she had just done. This happened every time she cleaned at that place. She wrote an email to the manager of her cleaning firm about it, but the only answer he had was that, well, maybe it was just noises from the building next door. That was probably it... these old buildings have funny echoes. But one time, she said, she heard the person above, she could hear their feet on the floor clear as anything, and it was too much. She'd had enough. The girl ran up the stairs to catch them, because she had to know, desperately, what was happening to her. They were still making noise as she ascended the stairs, growing louder and louder until she got to the top floor. The noise was coming from a room at the end of the landing. The door to that room was shut. She called, "is anybody there?", and nobody answered, of course. She walked down the landing, shaking, just a little bit. The door was locked, but she had a set of keys, one for every door in the building, or so she'd been told. There was still noise coming from inside the room. A long, agonising scrape as some item of furniture was pulled across the wooden floor. An unidentifiable thumping, and footsteps moving back and forth. At one point, she heard those footsteps get closer and closer to the door, and she looked down at her hands to see that they were shaking uncontrollably, before the steps moved away again, over to the other side of the room. She had cleaned this room in the past. She knew that one of these keys worked, but she couldn't remember exactly which one. There were small silver keys on the ring, and big, bronze-coloured ones, strange little ones that opened the bins out at the back of the building. Keys of every type. She wished she had made a note of which one worked for this, the last door, but she hadn't. That could have been it. The girl could have left the noise a mystery. But... when she told me this story, I asked that. Why open the door? Why did you need to see what was in there? She shrugged, and said she wasn't really sure, beyond the fact that this was her *workplace*, she felt unsafe, and she had to know why. So, the girl tried every key on the set, and, of course, they all stuck in the lock. Sometimes they stuck fast, and she had to pull hard to get them out again. This happened every time, until she came to the last one, which was big, golden. She put it in the lock, her breath rattling in and out. Then, at the last moment before she turned the key, she pulled it back out. She couldn't do this. She wasn't strong enough. But she still wanted to see... she bent down, so that her face was at the height of the keyhole, and peered through.

Do you know what was in there? Do you? Do you want to know? I know what you want to know and maybe what you want it to be, because I've spent a lot of time thinking about this, trying to reconstruct the circumstances of a haunting in my mind, and you want it to be nothing in there. You want her to look through the keyhole and find it empty, and then open the door with the key. You want her to walk around the room but find nothing out of place or strange in there at all. You want her to go to each wall and place her hand on the red wallpaper and feel a throb inside. Maybe see shapes in the old stains on the wallpaper. In all honesty, I would also like that to be what happened in the story. I asked for stories about hauntings to feel less alone, to feel less like an outsider from everybody around me. But that isn't what she found. Instead, she found a woman in there, who had been cleaning out her desk. This was her last day and she didn't want to leave things looking like a mess. She apologised for any distress she may have caused.

It feels like an anecdote that was meant to describe something, a metaphor about late capitalism, hauntology, about how work turns us all into ghosts, repeating the same learned actions over and over again for eternity. For that person, the wonder and the possibility and the horror of a haunting was just, in the end, somebody else doing their job for them.

The other thing is that this anticlimactic event only explained that one particular instance of hearing the noise. It did not explain all the other times that there had been sounds of somebody else in the building. There can't have been somebody moving out of those offices every single time she had a shift there, surely? She didn't sleep well when she thought about that. The girl told me that, afterwards, she requested to be moved to clean somewhere else. Every time she entered that building and looked up at those stairs, she felt queasy.

I have to believe that other people have also experienced impossible, horrible things.

I have to know that there are people who would understand if I talked to them. I have to know. I have to believe that my trauma is relatable, if controversial, that there are people who would listen to me and go, it's okay Alice, it's completely okay. You are so *fucking* normal. Everything you've experienced is normal. But soberly I think that, really, the only person out there who could ever understand is Ila, and I can't talk to her. I just can't. We used to be so close, but I can barely think about her now without having an anxiety attack. It's probably the same with her. I don't know for sure, but going from the sort of things she says now, if she thinks about me at all it is to hate me. I tried to be brave. She was a guest, recently, on a program on BBC Radio 4, and I really did try to sit and listen, as a form of exposure therapy. I turned it off after five minutes. I'd heard enough, and I had to smoke a joint to stop myself from passing out. Ila probably wants me to die. That's okay. I don't want her to die. I hate her, yes, I despise her with all my soul, in ways that it is hard to put into words, but I don't want her to die. I'm a good, forgiving person, I'm lovely. I live in this flat in this terrace house with all these hateful angles, and they remind me of another house, with other angles, angles that hate you more than it is even possible to comprehend, angles that crawl inside your brain and inside your body and move you around of their own accord, that make you see, think and feel things that nobody should ever have to see, think, feel, know, believe in. Angles that indicate the building you are in is not even really a building, that no human could have possibly thought of this when building it, that this house simply came into being from contact with the pure, violent terror that can only exist in the very worst examples of humanity. And that horror is transmitted through you, a little thing inside the heart of the place. It cuts its way into your body, or uses somebody else to cut its way into your body. I have a scar on my forehead to attest to that, and Ila has a scar on her stomach. And Hannah. Something happened to Hannah. The place, it worms into your brain and your heart. By the time I got out, I was different. The me who sits here right now in my room isn't the same me that went to University, went to all those parties, met a girl called Ila.

Ruined her. Got ruined by her.

My room isn't big. It's just too large to not be cosy, but not large enough to be spacious, in Estate Agent terms. When I moved in, I found a mark in the paint of the wall opposite my bed that I could have sworn hadn't been there when I viewed the flat. I took a picture of it and made sure to send it to the landlord, so he didn't try to charge me for it later when I needed to move out. I couldn't work out what the mark actually was, and it unsettled me, so I covered it up with a poster for a band that were popular a long time ago, before I was born. In the poster, four boys stand in front of a brick building. One of the boys is centred, the frontman of the band. The overwhelming personality, eclipsing the other three with ease. His hair sticks up, and he holds a branch in one hand sprouting white flowers. His heart aches. You broke his heart. He's miserable, and he sings about how everything makes him miserable. The meat industry, it makes him miserable. I don't know why I had the poster, honestly. I used to love the band... I still love the band. But I don't remember where the poster came from, it was just there, amongst all my stuff when I moved in here. So I put it up on the wall, over the blemish in the paint, thinking that would solve everything.

This was a mistake. After living here for about a month, my sleep started to dry up. That was it, at first, but I could feel that something was coming, and there was nothing I could do. Then he started to appear. Sometimes, at night, in the dark, when I can't know for sure if I am sleeping or lucid, the man, the one with the hair and the jawline, he crawls out from the poster, he stands over my bed, the flowers still in his hand, and he flickers in and out of focus. He pushes out from the past, away from his bandmates and into the now. He wants me. After this happened a couple of times, I blacked out his eyes with biro. Now, when he leaves the poster, he has no eyes, which looks terrifying but isn't as terrifying as it was when he *had* eyes. Think about it – think about the man, the one you picture in your head, with *eyes*. Stop and think about that for a moment.

When I moved in, I burned sage (after turning off the fire alarms), I made pieces of paper with my own private inventions drawn upon them and put one under each piece of furniture. Underneath my bed I placed a sheet with five black ink intersecting circles, which represented the boundaries of the room, the building, my physical body, the astral plane and my soul, which now must be saved. Inside the circle for my soul was an italicised *a* which represented my attempts at repressing my own trauma. This is a sort of private spell; not a legitimate charm of any kind, but one which I invented to control my own hauntings, or at least to try and control them. Maybe it does nothing at all. But it's good to feel in control of your environment. Of course, sometimes the singer still exits the poster and stands there, without sight, shifting. If I lay very, very still I know he will not come near me. I don't know what would happen if he came near me, but I know that I don't want to find out. The closest he has come is there at the end of my bed. I think maybe, if he did approach me, he would try to black out my eyes. With a pen, if he could find one. Maybe he would try to do it even without a pen, maybe he would do it with his fingers, pushing them into my eyes, singing the whole time, not singing properly, opening his mouth and having the songs come out without him moving his lips for the words, like there is a speaker inserted into his throat that plays when he opens his mouth, pushing his thumbs into my eyes, *last truly British people*, and when he is done with my eyes he would grab my mouth to put his words into it, *panic on the-*, whilst images of imagined atrocities that he has made up play in my head. A van, swerving sharply into a crowd of police officers, crushing their bones beneath its wheels. A man suddenly rising up on the tube, swaying a little with the motion of movement before running down the length of the train, swinging a sword along a row of commuters. A man, anonymous, shooting at a pushchair. A teenage boy walking to the front of the class and cutting his teacher's throat with a knife. Two trans people walking together bold and defiant but then a bomb explodes next to them and their brains and their limbs scatter over the streets like snow. These images grow bloodier and bloodier until they are pure red and there are no figures in them at all, just dripping, wet redness. I become overwhelmed and throw up, realising that I cannot see, and cannot speak words that are not his, or think thoughts that are not his. This is what might happen if he comes to me. I have been careful to ensure that he can't get that close. I know how to protect myself. He can crawl out of the poster but he cannot come near me, because I know to lay very, very still, because I have placed the right sigils in the right places, which stop him from getting to my eyes and my mouth. Lay still. Hold your breath. Don't look at him directly. Let him retreat back into the picture.

I put on makeup for the first time in what must be a month. When it's not in use, the mirror on my desk is covered up with a flannel, and now I see how dirty the glass is, blotched with spots of sticky residue which have been gathering dust. I try to wash it, but only make it smeared. Through the blurriness, my face almost looks okay. I've shaved. I put on a turtleneck to hide my Adam's Apple. It's hard to get the symmetry of eyeliner right in the dirty glass; that's a job that requires a precision that, even with a clear mirror, I can't quite manage with the tremor that runs through my hands, so I opt to avoid eyeliner, cake my eyes in red powder, put a shiny lipstick on my lips that matches. Tie my hair – too long, scraggly – back into some semblance of neat femininity. I'm clockable, but that's okay. It's alright if you don't pass, a voice in me says. No one cares. The only people that care are people you don't want to be around anyway. But another part of me, a vicious little creature that claws at my head, calls me *a fucking brick sissy* whispers *everyone can see your stubble everyone is creeped out by you in the toilets.* I tell it to shut up, try to suppress it. It's the same part of me that looks at girls nervously sharing their selfies on Trans Day of Visibility and wants to spit bile through the screen. *You're sharing that picture of yourself? Everyone can see you're not a woman. Everyone knows.* A pale, nasty jealousy at their apparent unselfconsciousness. I don't ever vocalise this side of me, of course. These thoughts are intrusive. I do my best to suppress them.

There's a party which, against all odds, I've been invited to. There are a couple of people that I call friends, although I'm not really close with any of them, not in the way I was close with Ila and, to a lesser extent, Hannah. Ila and I had the kind of friendship where the frictions between two people soften enough that your boundaries blur. We couldn't have been more different, looking at us, but seminar leaders would still get us mixed up, to our delight. It's the opposite of when people think I'm some other brown girl, Ila used to say, or when they say you look like that model, despite the fact that you totally don't, like at all. The friends who invited me to the party, a quick text at midday today, aren't like that with me. But they're fine. I've been basically a shut-in for ages now, so it's good to go to places with people that don't completely hate your guts.

I get the bus across town to the address Jon texted to me – with a note saying to get there at *about ten* because things will be really happening by then. The air outside is cold and the foxes are out at the bins at the end of my road, tearing at black plastic bags, barking their strange, human screams. I steer clear of them, and wait for the bus, which, when it arrives, is busier than I expected. Full of other people, going to other parties, some of them already drunk. I'm not drunk yet, I had a couple of glasses of red wine sat on my bed listening intently to Darkthrone and trying to calm my nerves, but it hasn't hit me. Not with the same force that pre-drinks have hit a lot of the partygoers on the bus. When I go to sit down I realise that the seat is wet with something, vomit, splattered across the fabric and down onto the floor. A boy sat at the back of the bus lights a cigarette and fills the inside with smoke. The driver stops the bus, and says, over the intercom, that whoever is smoking has to put it out right now or he'll call the police. The boy throws the fag out of the bus window, and on we go. The boy loudly calls the driver a word that makes me wince, and I wonder if I should say something. Hey, you. Don't say that. Is it worth exposing myself to violence for the easing of my own white guilt? It's not like I'm safe. If he realises what I am, he might turn his attention to me. It's safety, pure and simple, that's all. You have to look out for yourself. The whole bus smells like vomit and alcohol and smoke, encasing my brain in the stench. Welcome back to the real world. There are no singers pushing out from posters to haunt you here, but there is piss and vomit and men talking too loudly, enough to make your nerves tight.

I get off the bus at about twenty to ten, find a bench at the end of the same street the party's on, and wait until it seems appropriate for me to arrive. The hosts don't know me, only Jon and Sasha, and Leon, their twink trans guy coke addict friend, know who I am. I can't turn up and say that they invited me if they aren't there yet, the social embarrassment would stick in my gut. In my coat pocket, there's a packet of Gold Leaf tobacco, so I roll a cigarette, thinking about the smoking boy on the bus, hoping he didn't also smoke Gold Leaf. I finish smoking, stuff the yellow filter in between the wooden planks that make up the bench, and roll another. By the time that's done, I retch, dryly, until the feeling of nausea in my throat from smoking two cigarettes in a row goes away, and I stand up, getting balance. The party isn't far from here. It's five to ten at night and I can't see the moon or the stars, but I know they're there beyond the smog and the light pollution.

I have the number of the house, but I won't need it – all the houses on the street are quiet, many of them empty, holiday rentals in the off-season. This is close to the sea, after all. But one of the houses is alive and as I get closer, I can feel bass thumping through the pavement. The blinds are down in the windows, but I can see silhouettes of people pressed close through them, pink light shining out. It looks busy, and loud.

It's not too late for me to go. I'm cold, I've had some wine. I could just go home. Maybe I could get some sleep. The singer might not appear tonight. Just as I've decided to turn back, get the bus all the way home, I hear a voice shout "Hey, Alice!". Jon is walking towards me, Sasha and Leon close in tow. Sasha's white face peers through a bundle of fake fur, blue eyeliner sharp and pointed nearly to her brows. She tried to teach me how to do that once, but I shook too much. Jon looks like he has rich parents, and he does, richer than mine, one's a lawyer I think and the other has a senior position at the *Guardian*. He doesn't *sound* rich though, there's an affected edge to his voice, Ts dropped as often as he can. Until he gets really drunk, or really high, or both. Then that clipped BBC English comes out swinging. He's not there yet though.

"Hey, Alice, how're ya?"

It seems mocking, but I can't tell who it's meant to be mocking.

"I'm okay," I say.

"Been busy?"

I laugh. "Good one, Jon. You?"

He shrugs. "Been working a lot."

Yeah, right...

Sasha comes to me and we hug. The fake fur coat she's wearing is unbelievably soft, I want to just settle into it and sleep for an eternity, but then she breaks the embrace.

"You look pretty!" she says, really meaning it.

"Got any gear?" asks Leon.

"Jesus, that was quick. You didn't even say hello."

"Nah," he says. "You need to have drugs on you to get into the party."

"Ah, shit, really?" I have a little Ziploc bag of pills back in my makeup box at the flat, but I thought I wouldn't be doing anything tonight. Shit.

"It's okay," says Jon, "I've got like, two extra bags of MD and a bag of Ket that I don't need." I hesitate. "You don't have to use, just give it back to me once we're in, y'know."

He holds three bags of identical white powder out to me in the palm of his hand, and I take one at random, not knowing if it's MD or Ket and not caring. He must have already given some to Sasha, and Leon is probably always carrying anyway. Cops never stop him. He's small, they mistake him for a white girl, they don't care, why would they? We exchange curt nods, the sort of acknowledgement you do to one another when you are the only trans people in a situation. Maybe there'll be more of us at the party, I don't know the crowd, but probably not.

Jon leads us up the stairs to the house's front door. It's a big, ugly townhouse. It hides how old it is, it hides its secrets well. When the door opens, the man standing there says something to Jon that I can't hear because suddenly the music and the voices from inside are deafening. But Jon holds up one of his white bags, and the host nods. I do the same. The man at the door is only a little older than me. He must live here. He looks at me, looks at my body, looks at the white powder in the bag in my hand, then nods and smiles. I step through the door, hoping that the noise will get less bad once it surrounds me. It doesn't.

I'm not a party person much now. They used to be my thing, especially over clubs. That's definitely still true, but I also find them disorienting. They feel dangerous. All these people I don't know packed into one space, thick with bodies. If a crowd turns on you, where can you go? I push through the hot sweaty treacle of the air, sliding between people I don't know, following Jon, who seems to be walking with purpose. I turn around. Sasha has taken off her fur coat. Otherwise she'd be boiling to death already. I don't know the music that's playing, it's asynchronous, jarring electronic noises that throw themselves at the walls with the force of a person running. The people I push past look at me like I'm an invasive species.

Jon has found the coat room, which is just somebody's bedroom with coats and bags piled up on the bed and on the shelves chaotically. I put my coat under the bed, which is probably not where someone wanting to steal things would look. My jeans have pockets anyway, for my phone and my tobacco and keys. We head back out into the party and find a space to dance in one of the larger rooms with a speaker. Leon is already high, he can't talk much. I try to dance with him, and he offers me poppers. I accept. Take a deep breath of liquid from the little bottle he holds under my nose. Throw my head back, stumble a little, put my hand against someone I don't know for balance. Feel my brain floating for a couple of seconds, suspended in the air. My asshole opening. Like a flower of evil from Baudelaire. And then my awareness comes crashing back down. Fuck, I think, I want drugs. I didn't give the bag back to Jon, maybe he won't even know. I huddle close to Leon, tell him to be still for a moment while I snort crystalline powder off of the end of the key to my flat, fuck, fuck, fuck I missed this, I remember this, I used to do this with Ila. Leon looks at me like I said something horrible and I realised I'd just said that out loud. "I used to do this with Ila."

"Who's Ila?" he asks.

"Ah, um. My ex." It's not the truth.

People are smoking inside, but I need cold air in my lungs and on my face, so I push my way through the kitchen and out into the garden. Jon and Sasha are there, both smoking straights, talking to a girl I haven't seen before. Immediately my alarm bells ring. They're probably trying to get her to be a unicorn. I found their shared Tinder once: *J + S looking for female third who enjoys good food good drinks and good company*. I don't care what people do, obviously, but I know Jon can get weird and freak people out. He's not dangerous or anything. He has a bit of an edgy sense of humour. Sometimes he makes jokes that land badly about the holocaust, and strangers can get pissed off. Plus, there's the knife thing. He likes knives. He told me this, once. We'd been joking but suddenly he got all serious. "Is it like, weird," he said, "to like holding a knife to a girl? To get off on it? Not hurt her or anything, obviously I do it with, ah, consent, but. I'm worried." I told him it wasn't weird at all. Afterwards, he got out a knife, and, laughing, held it first to Sasha's throat, caressing her nervous smile with his other hand, then to my throat. The blade was cold against my Adam's Apple. He pressed it in, too hard. Just for a moment. He didn't mean anything by it, but I panicked. I couldn't stop thinking about... about Ila, standing over me. I'm never even sure if I do remember that, or if somebody just told me what happened.

I have a scar on my forehead, which I cover with a fringe. Most people don't see it.

Jon didn't know that I'd freak out. And he apologised, later. Said he'd never do it again, honest.

The girl they're talking to is tall, and her hair is impossibly shiny. There's a jewelled piercing in her nose and another on her lip. I slip in, between her and Jon and Sasha, as a buffer. The girl smiles at me. "Hi there," she says. "God..." she stops for a moment, looking at my face intensely, then says, "Sorry, I just had to do that." She steps back, scanning me up and down. "You're stunning," she smiles. I don't really know what to say, so I tell her she is very beautiful. I give her a smile that appears shy but that we both know really isn't. I don't really allow myself to get close to people on an emotional level because my insides are all riddled with maggots, which is very frightening for people to see, especially up close, especially when they are, you know, inside you, in more ways than one. But I try to fuck well. And I try to be charming, partly because I'm scared that if I go too far into being drawn-off and distant it'll seem like I'm a fuckboy, like, a man, or like I'm treating people like a man treats women, and I'm very scared to be seen like that. That's why I always sit down to pee in public bathrooms, because people might see my feet under the stall standing up. And I don't talk too much, because men talk too much, with too much confidence. So, there's a thin line between being careful but not distant. Or at least, there is a line between being distant and seeming distant.

Me and the girl find our way back inside. More specifically, she grabs my hand and pulls me back into the house, back amongst the tangled limbs of the party. The building has been gutted and refitted to be fit for students, but the shell of it is old. Old enough to be haunted or, if not, perhaps whatever was on this site before was haunted. Sometimes the ghosts from old buildings stay around to see what comes next. Every spot on the planet has something in its past that is worth haunting about. Or if, miraculously, it does not, then there's always the future, which holds far worse for everyone. It haunts backwards. Things from the future, pushing back into the now because they are so utterly traumatic that they can't stay within the limits of the time, they have to be happening now, around you. To you. There's a type of storm coming.

The girl shouts over the music that her name is Sabi. I offer her some of the drugs, and she doesn't ask what they are, she just takes a bump from her key, and then, just as I've stashed the drugs away, she kisses me, out of nowhere. I nearly fall back against the people behind me.

I haven't even been here long but I try to find Jon, at least, to say that I'm leaving. He sees me, and sees Sabi holding my hand, and grins. "Get it," he says. I roll my eyes.

The bus journey back is a blur of making out on the seats, and boys shouting, but not at me, not at us, we're safe.

Now I'm in my apartment, and I'm trying very hard to climb inside this girl, suddenly, trying to push into the space in which she is. I want to be safe, in there, in the warmth of someone else. When we left the party I'd asked Sabi if we could go to hers instead, but she said she lives with her parents so that wasn't really possible. Now we're lying in my bed. She has her head on my chest, and she's staring out into the abyss of my bedroom.

"Can you... take that down?" she asks, motioning vaguely towards the poster opposite.

"Why?"

"That guy... he's, like, racist," she mumbles.

She's right. Shit, I didn't even think how it might look, having the poster of him up there. Shit.

When someone calls you racist, thinks the thing inside the poster, *what they are saying is "Hmm, you actually have a point, and I don't know how to answer it."* The spirit in the poster is angry at this accusation. It wants to lash out. It pulses, in the picture, wanting to tear at the fabric of reality. I can feel it already, across the room.

"Fuck, yeah," I say, "I'm sorry, I didn't really think. He was very important to me when I was younger."

I extract myself from Sabi's arms and walk across the room, naked, trying not to think about what my weird, pale, flabby naked body looks like while I move. I pull the poster down, but I'm careful not to tear it. Pulling it down does not actually rob it of its power, because whatever is here is deep inside now, like how a tick's head stays dug deep into you when you pick its body off. There's no use in pulling down this poster beyond the symbolic. Not that the symbolic is of no use, of course. The symbolic can be vital, the symbolic can evict or restore power. Symbols hold a shocking potential energy deep within, sometimes not evoked for generations upon generations. When I take the poster down, I see that the mark on the wall beneath it appears to have grown, from a tiny spot into a blotch. *Getting closer,* I think, but I don't know why. I can't say what it is that is getting closer. The thought vanishes as soon as it arrived, and I put the poster under my bed, in the dark space where I put things that I cannot deal with. Under there, too, are pictures of Ila and I, holding hands looking at the sunrise, pictures taken by Hannah on a little disposable camera. I can't look at them, but I can't bear to throw them out. The sigils down in the dark there too are supposed to keep things safe. I am not always sure they work as I hoped.

Sabi looks at me. "Thank you," she says, and puts her arms around me.

I pour us each a glass of wine from a bottle on my bedside table, and we sit on my bed.

"Have you lived here long?" she asks.

"No, not really. I mean I've been in the city for a few years, but I move house a lot, I can never seem to settle in a place, really. I'm... a restless thing."

She laughs. "A thing?"

"Not a thing, haha, you – you know what I mean."

She touches me, and her arms are real arms, I think, I feel real arms. She looks into my eyes. "How do you want me to treat your body?" she asks.

The question takes me by surprise. I remember once

sleeping with a girl who insisted on referring to my penis as a "pussy." *I'm going to suck your pussy now*, she said, crawling towards me over her parent's sofa. She's dead now. She killed herself about a year ago. I got a strange message from her a week before she died, and it seemed like she didn't know what country she was in.

Sometimes, very occasionally, she is here too, with the eyeless singer from the poster, standing next to him and whispering about me being a beautiful little doll. But I have to admit that I don't think she is really there. I think she's just a symptom of the thing in the poster's presence. She has no business being here, this isn't her place, this isn't her pussy, even if she used to touch me and say, this is my (her) pussy, you are mine (hers), I am not her doll, her muse, her plaything. In any case, she never stays for long, which is how I know she is only a momentary spasm of the soul.

Beneath the bed, the man in the poster hears and feels Sabi and I fucking, although it can't see it.

Her finger traces my scar again when we lay in the sweaty aftermath. I didn't cum. Sabi asks, what happened, in a sleepy, off-puttingly romantic tone.

"I was attacked by a friend." Sabi looks horrified. "She, uh, I don't really know. This isn't really the right way of saying it, but it was like she went insane."

I'm not sure how true that statement is. Ila would say that it was me who went insane. Maybe I am too easy on her.

"It would have been hard to continue to exist," I say, carefully, "in the place we were and not break."

Because. Because... okay, let me describe it like this, in a way that can be understood. No live organism can continue to exist compassionately under conditions of absolute fascism, even the pigs in Chile under Pinochet's rule were observed to take part in political killings. The House, not compassionate, stood ringed by a thick, angry forest, holding inside, however messily, its overpowering ideology; it had stood so for a hundred years and would stand for three more. Inside, the hallways were as still and empty as a frozen lake, and the walls found themselves leaning in different directions depending on who they hated the most that day. Sometimes, animals would wander into the House, but they never wandered out again. Whoever owned it did not seem to care for it, so we, Ila, Hannah and I, decided we'd break in and spend a night there. Young people can be stupid. We wanted to make some political point of the whole thing, we disagreed that great old houses like this should be empty when there were homeless people on every street. We knew that the owner might send people to pull us out, but we wanted to prove something. We were young and idealistic. The House stood on the outskirts of a city, with a huge DANGER KEEP OUT sign across the rusted gates. The fence, however, had decayed, so we bypassed the gates and crossed the boundaries easily. Nobody was around.

I first read *The Haunting of Hill House* when I was sixteen, and I've never been able to think about hauntings since then in a way that didn't align with that book's idea of a fundamentally demented place onto which you latch. Our house, my house, her house, was not like Hill House, however much

I structure my thoughts on it in the same way. Hill House was, I think, an apolitical animal. Our house was not. It had a system of beliefs. And those who walked there marched as one faceless mass.

I wake up to a loud thump, feeling it underneath me. Sabi is sitting up in bed, with the covers pulled up to her chin, and her eyes wide and manic.

"Was that the door?" I ask sleepily. I know it wasn't. I felt the thump, physically. And then there's another one, even harder this time. My brain rushes towards lucidity, and I realise that it is not the door, or the wall, or the ceiling. It's coming from beneath us, from underneath the bed, where it hides in the dark with all those pictures of Ila and I, along with unopened letters from the bank and from the gender clinic, down there with the repressed things, and now it is trying to push up against the ceiling it found when it reached out, trying to push it away so it can rise to the surface. The man in the poster. The thing inside the man in the poster. Flowers gently in his hand. I sit up and pull Sabi close to me.

"It's underneath us," I say, quietly.

"It?"

"Don't move or it will... I don't know, just don't move. Shh now, quiet."

The thumping stops, leaving a momentary, cold silence. I wonder if that's it. Maybe it retreated back to its bandmates, to sing mournfully about lost love and growing up lonely, but then there's a *scraping*. I can feel it beneath me on the underside of the bed. The noise of sharp fingernails against wood fills the air. We fall back together and press close as the bed starts, slowly, to slide to the left. Sabi screams, I have to put my hand over her mouth to get her to stop. She hits me, hard, with the back of her hand.

"Get off me!" she says. I try to grab her in panic, trying to stop her from doing what she is about to do. I miss, and she jumps from the bed, onto the floor.

"You're fucking insane," she says, "you're fucking insane."

As she stands there looking at me like I'm the worst thing in the world, a pale hand appears from the gap underneath the bed. She doesn't see it. I point to it, trying to warn her, but before she can look down it grabs onto her ankle. Sabi screams again, and the hand jerks her to the ground and across the floor towards the dark space where the man in the poster hides with sightless eyes and an open mouth spurting a melodic voice. Sabi scrabbles at the floor with her fingers but there's nothing to hold onto. I can hear him singing, as if this isn't my bedroom, as if he isn't a spirit inhabiting a poster of a man who isn't even dead. He's singing like he's at Finsbury Park. He's singing like England is for the English, he's singing and pulling at Sabi, Sabi is screaming, I am screaming at him to let her go, let go of her, let her go... I jump off the bed after her and put my arms around her waist. His pull is strong, eating at her, england for the english, england for the english, panic but england for the english I wear black on the outside 'cause this is not your country and – now a hand from nowhere appears and claps over my mouth. I hear a woman whisper that this, here, this is her pussy, I'm a little doll and she is going to paint me, I look up at her and see a pale face bent strangely, her neck is broken, and I am her broken little pussy, abnormal and wet. I don't let go of Sabi, though. My arms are locked around her. I can't see anything. The man in the poster can't see, because I blacked out his eyes, thank fucking God I blacked out his eyes. My dead ex-girlfriend can see me, but she's barely real, she's only here because the membrane of repression has broken, she can be pushed back down into the mud, but her neck is broken, and she wants to break mine. Not the real girl, you understand, she would never have broken my neck. I don't think. I don't know. She did hurt me once but. It is whatever is inside the memory of her now, whatever that is, maybe it's me, maybe I am haunting myself, maybe I have always been haunting myself. I exist under conditions of the absolute. If you cut a cunt into my forehead, what is that for, who is getting the power there, you do it to tease me, here's what you want but not how you want it, here's what you want me to do but I do it all wrong. You can tell me ghosts aren't real all you like, but rooms are real, they have real walls with angles that hold suggestions cut deep into the blueprints, and sometimes, in those blueprints, someone has hidden your childhood hero in the walls, with no chance of exorcism. I feel the pull on Sabi go slack. I loosen my hold. She runs away from me, for the door.

"You're insane," she shouts at me again. And underneath the bed, the singer's face peers out from the darkness, but the darkness is his eyes and he fades away into it. There is no longer a hand over my mouth. There is no longer anything. The door opens, and Sabi is gone. I am going to stay here all night. This is going to happen forever. Ila is somewhere else, dreaming of single-sexed bathrooms. I miss Hannah, I miss her screaming along to songs with filthy lyrics, shaking her hair until it was wild. I miss her screaming in the rotting redness, with her limbs askew. I can try to make my limbs askew if I work hard at it. I'm not very flexible, true, but I can work hard at it. I'll get better for Hannah.

I stand up, my legs shaking, and see that Sabi has left her phone on my bedside table, next to the half-drunk bottle of wine. I put on some clothes and shoes, the same ones I had worn out earlier, although they feel strangely cold and damp now, in the wee small hours of the morning. I grab her phone and run after her, hoping that she hasn't vanished.

She's outside, sitting on the curb, shaking. "You left your phone," I say from behind her.

She doesn't react. Above, a bat loops around the street-light, pulling moths out of the air with its little teeth. And the foxes are still there, at the bins, rubbish strewn across the tarmac. Sabi looks up at me, and I have no idea what she sees. I hold out her phone to her, though, and she takes it.

"What the fuck was that?" she asks, but I can tell she is not looking for a real answer.

I leave Sabi on the street, but make sure she's called a taxi.

I walk into my flat, which feels frozen. I carefully go over to the bed and pull the poster out from under there.

You are wondering why I don't tear the poster to pieces. Why I didn't do that before, and why I don't do it now. Yes, there is a temptation for me to tear him up. But if I did that, who knows what the spirits would try to force their way inside next. I can't keep everything at bay forever. Perhaps, without the poster, the haunting would finally come into me, after threatening to do so for years. I can imagine that happening. I lie on the bed. I can feel the rough sheets. I've hung the poster, the singer with his serious sad face, back on the wall where he belongs, now England, as he says, is his. England... I'm happy to have him there, within view again. I don't want to hide all the bad things away beneath my bed like a kid asked to tidy his room. Like the British Empire.

There's no chance of me sleeping any more. I open my laptop to watch a dumb comedy about American cops. They don't act like real cops; they act like what a child thinks a cop acts like. At the same time, I look at my phone. On the screen, a Jewish man chases a criminal, quipping as the criminal falls down a flight of stairs. On my phone, I see an email notification.

It's from Ila.

This happens every couple of months, but I never get used to it. I jump up, away from my phone and my laptop, and run to the bathroom, nearly tripping over my own feet on the way. Jesus Christ, how fucking dare she. How fucking dare she message me, trying to talk to me. After everything she did, everything she said. I can hear the theme tune of the sitcom playing jauntily as I throw up into the sink. My vomit is pure alcohol. I heave it out of me, and then press my head on the cold ceramic of the sink for a few moments to get my breath back before more sick pushes its way up out of my throat. Even when I've brought up everything I can, I keep being sick, throwing up nothing apart from air and strings of bile. Eventually this stops, and I collapse in relief. There's a rush of feeling through my head. I stay there, panting, looking into the light on the ceiling, letting it burn my eyes a little bit. After a while, I pull myself to my feet, and lean my head against the rim of the sink again. I lift it up slightly. I knock my head against the sink, just hard enough to hurt me a little bit. Fuck you. You fucking horrible thing. You will never get away. You will always be in the same room forever. You had potential and now look at you. Haunted by an old racist man. I knock my head against the sink. The pain is good. It cleanses the rising panic. I do it again, the sharp noise of it bringing me a base pleasure. Again. Again. Each time I go a little harder. Eventually, if I keep at this, either I or the sink will break, and there will be a cleansing flood to wash through me, through the bathroom, through the whole fucking flat.

ILA

This is a therapy.

The streets are littered with crisp packets, and seagulls with evil little black eyes peck at them derangedly. They make her nervous. They get violent, here, she's had them snatch sandwiches directly from her fingers, she's seen them scratch at people's faces. Big, white winged beasts, calling their ugly calls high above the roofs and then dropping to the earth to hunt for waste. She walks up the slight incline of the hill, past an old church here with boarded up plywood on the windows, and a sign outside reading TRESPASSERS WILL BE PROSECUTED. God's body, decaying, has now been cut off from society; do not touch him, for he is owned by a variety of contractors, and they have legal power over the likes of you.

Her phone buzzes. It's an unknown number, saying *lots of resistance. use side entrance.*

Ila is nervous. She can admit that to herself. Her heart is beating too fast, and her breathing is too fast as well. At any moment she could trip over her own feet. Someone would probably see and laugh at her. The place must be close now; she gets out her phone and checks the map, sees that yes, it's on the next street over, but this route leads to the main entrance, which is no use now she's been directed, for her own safety, to the side entrance, wherever that is. It's close enough now that she can hear loud, angry voices, tuneless chants calling into the wind that "Trans rights are human rights! Trans rights are human rights!" As Ila gets closer, turns the street, trying to work out how to get around the crowd and into the back, the chanting gets louder. She turns the street again and there they are. They haven't seen her yet, or, at least, they haven't worked out that she isn't just some random passer-by, or even a stranger, maybe a resident, curious about the noise. She can see them all crowded around the building. They have pastel-coloured flags flying in the air, draped over their shoulders, blocking the pavement. They have to keep moving so they don't freeze to death in their dresses, dresses which are far too short. Dresses that she thinks no woman would wear. They look like little girls who grew up very suddenly and very wrong. This is a cruel thought, but she lets it sit there. There is a Grimm's fairy tale that she half remembers from childhood, about a chambermaid who steals a princess' life, after the princess loses a precious handker-chief spotted with three drops of blood. The princess can say nothing of her plight as she watches the chambermaid inhabit her entire identity, ride her horse, eat her rich foods, sleep in her soft silk beds. She meets the king, who the princess is supposed to wed. But the king discovers the ruse and asks the chambermaid, still believing her plan to have worked, what punishment a lady should incur for deceiving her king, to which the chambermaid says that the deceiver should strip completely naked and be put inside a barrel studded with sharp nails, then the barrel should be dragged by two white horses through the streets until she's dead. The king reveals that he knows the truth. The princess is freed, and the chambermaid is punished in the way she suggested: dragged through the streets in the spiked barrel until they pulled out her corpse, impaled again and again.

Seeing this crowd, these imposters in the guise of women, makes her feel like the princess looking upon the chambermaid. And she can't speak. To speak would be bigotry.

She skirts the crowd, on the other side of the street, trying to look like a nobody. The crowd thins as she turns around the building, but then she sees that the information that was texted to her was wrong, or at least not up to date. It's a smaller group of protestors, here at the back entrance, but they've spotted her, and they can tell. She knows they can tell. Under the grey sky, their colourful bright clothing looks ridiculously out of season. The edges of the crowd are peppered with policemen and policewomen, looking confused. They don't even know what this is. It's totally clear, nobody briefed them on the specifics, beyond that there was some kind of meeting and some kind of counterprotest to the meeting. Her eyes scan the group around the door, but Alice isn't there. She might still be with the other group, however. Fuck. What would she do, if she was here? If she had to see that face again?

And she thinks, also, about all those unanswered messages she's sent, and feels panic rising. Panic on the streets.

The crowd is chanting at the top of their lungs. When, if, she gets inside, she won't even be able to make herself heard properly. She'll have to write all of her words down on a whiteboard, or maybe scream them. If she screams her words that might make her seem hysterical. There's a quote from Avital Ronell's introduction to the *SCUM Manifesto* where she talks about Heidegger, the philosopher, feminising Nietzsche in a piece of writing and representing him as a hysterical bitch, and she always feels like that. Screaming to get her point across... and that's what the protestors are doing, too. Maybe that's why they really are women. Ila walks closer, trying to keep her head down, hidden partly under the thick scarf she wrapped around her neck and shoulders. Someone is taking photographs. The chanting is directed straight at her now, stabbing her all over as she walks closer to the group to try and get through. The cops have made sure there's a path through the angry, hissing transgenders, but it's a slim path, a fragile route. Ila puts her head down, not looking to either side, and follows it, trying to get to the door as quickly as she can, and from every side they scream at her. "Trans women are real women!" She bites her tongue. "Trans men are real men!" It's a tuneless, empty chant. Every other syllable is enunciated. "Non-binary is valid!" She actually laughs, a light nervous laugh, at that one, because it doesn't even fit the structure of their chant. They can't even get "non-binary" to fit into their own calls for action! The crowd is getting closer on both sides, and, for a moment she wonders what happens if they get to her. The cops are there, sure, but they're outnumbered. Could she run for it? Maybe, she doubts that there are any athletes amongst the group. But a crowd made of limbs and angry mouths can do so many things.

Finally, after what felt like far too long, she gets to the door, and opens it, into the warm, relatively safe inside of the building. Here, the crowd is still loud, but their monolithic, cult-like chanting is muffled, just a little bit. A smartly dressed young woman stands just inside, at a wooden table. She smiles at Ila warmly, but her eyes keep darting around the room with an anxious energy. They can't seem to settle on Ila.

"Hi," she says. "I'm Gemma. Did you get in okay?"

The protestors have started to bang with their fists on the windows. The noise is echoing, deep and arrhythmic. She feels like her body is this building, and they are kicking her windows, and this hurts. "I mean, it was okay as it could possibly be, I suppose. Have the police said anything?" Ila asks.

Gemma listens to the banging for a moment. "They aren't allowed to hit the windows like that."

"Well, they're doing it anyway," says Ila. "What happens if they break the glass?" The question stays in the air. Gemma says nothing.

Outside the building, a policeman approaches the crowd calmy. The crowd, a collection of trans people and cisgender allies from around the city, plus a few from elsewhere, is unresponsive to him. The policeman voted Lib Dem in the last election and thinks of himself as an ally.

"Excuse me," he calls at the protestors, the ones banging on the windows. "Protest all you like but you can't do that!" The protestors stop, but he can see them smirking at him, and wonders why.

The meeting is filling up, despite the resistance from the blockade. Ila looks around, and notices that, with a couple of exceptions, she's probably the youngest person here. A lot of the women have short, boyish haircuts, flecked with grey. Many look like academics. It's hard to say what the academic look is, but Ila has seen enough tenured professors in her life to recognise the way they dress, the way they hold themselves. A sort of satisfied look on their faces. I made it; I did the impossible. That sort of look. Ila walks up to the refreshments table and pours herself a glass of red wine, although her hand isn't steady.

This building itself is, apparently, the Black and Minority Ethnic Community centre, although Ila lives here, considers herself a member of the BAME community, and hasn't ever heard of it before, let alone been here. It doesn't escape her that almost every woman in this meeting, apart from her, is white. There are a few white men milling around too, here and there. She wonders sometimes if she is being tokenised and used as a shield against accusations of racism from the trans crowd. She probably is. It's an inescapable fact of being involved in political action. People want you, yes, but not for you. No, they just like how you look in the press photos. A lot of these women only care about protecting women's sex-based rights as an academic exercise, when this is actually a very material argument, one that affects, infects, and infests public life. This is not simply a thought experiment. She rubs her stomach, absentmindedly. It itches often but is rarely genuinely painful. There is a war on women being fought in public toilets across this country, and she needs to piss.

She leaves her glass of wine on the table and goes to the women's toilets. The room is starkly modern. The walls are yellow, and the toilet stalls feel like escape pods from a spaceship. She locks herself in one, and sits down to piss a long, satisfying stream into the toilet bowl. When she's done, she takes her wine glass into the conference room. She stands outside, a little away from everyone else, holding her wine firmly, and goes through a mindfulness exercise in her head. *I can smell perfume. I can see people. I can hear the crowd... no, ignore that. I can hear people pleasantly talking. I can taste this cheap red wine. I can feel the glass in my hand. I am calm. I am correct. I am okay. This is a therapy.*

Ila doesn't see ghosts. If she does, she tries not to look, and instead looks around them. In her flat, she has a little balcony with plants on, and when it's warm she likes to sit out there and smoke weed as the sun sets. She left the Labour Party due to what she saw as their ignorance on women's rights issues. Her scars no longer show as much as they once did. You have to look, carefully, to see most of them. There is one on her upper thigh, a cut that looks like a word, although it's unclear what it actually says. She doesn't remember making the cut, and she wonders if, in fact, she didn't make it at all. In the bath, she sits and looks at her thigh and tries to decipher it. A lover, post-coital, once traced her finger along it idly, and told her she thought it said *panic*.

Ila walks into the room. The meeting should be starting soon, but the crowd is still loud, making conversation difficult at best. They have stopped hitting the windows, at least. The blinds have been pulled down but, through the gaps, she can see the protesters outside, their faces and bodies pressed close up against the glass. One of the women, with short grey hair, strides purposefully up to the window, although it is unclear what she was planning on doing, and in any case, another woman, also with short grey hair, grabs her and convinces her to sit back down.

"We should start," shouts Gemma over the din.

Ila thought Gemma was just working there, not actually involved in the proceedings. In actual fact, Gemma is neither working nor properly involved, but has instead inserted herself there as a mole. She just texted somebody outside that they need to start singing louder because things are starting properly, and they do, they start chanting even louder than before, loud enough to vibrate the glass in the windows and the legs of the seats.

Gemma introduces the evening. Originally, there had been hope that she might be able to get the protesters into the building itself, but it became clear that the legality of doing this would have been tenuous. But she's able to leak information, which is better than nothing. None of the people in the room have even clocked that she's actually transgender and has lived happily as a woman since her late teens. Three years from now, she will test positive for breast cancer, having not thought to get tested because it didn't seem possible that a trans woman would be able to develop it. She will have to have her left breast removed. Her breasts had begun to grow at about twenty, and now she's thirty-two, and suddenly there she will be, feeling the angry pain of teenage dysphoria all over again concentrated on the left of her chest where there is now a curved scar that she thought was ugly. However, through advances in medical technology, as well as the loving support of her friends, Gemma will live a long and happy life. She will be marching in the parade during the 2028 Pride Bombing, but will suffer only superficial injuries, whereas others standing close to her on that day will be killed in the explosion.

After Gemma, women, one by one, come up to speak on why this fight matters to them, on how they see this current war on women, but it is all fairly pointless because the protestors are shouting loud enough that all these women's words are flattened into vague noise. A woman comes up to talk, with a shock of spiky black hair, clearly dyed. Her face is wrinkled like a pale tree's bark. Ila tries to concentrate on what she's saying, which is something vague about academic freedom, two words that make Ila roll her eyes. Too many of the people here only care about academic freedom. She wants to scream, first at the people outside to *shut the fuck up* so she can hear herself think, but then she wants to scream at the people in this room to listen to her, to please *listen* to what she is saying, to think about what this all means, the fact that it is materially affecting her body, that she will find herself, if this keeps happening, in some toilet, panicking because there is somebody in there who breaks the social contract of who you should be when you come into the fucking women's toilets, who has deluded themselves into thinking they belong. And even if they stay private and respectful, as she's sure most trans people really are, the simple fact they are there makes her unsafe.

Gemma was in the toilet at the same time as her, just now. After Ila realised she had to piss, Gemma had followed her in. She was shitting in one of the stalls while Ila pissed, and Ila hadn't noticed, or cared.

Outside, things have degraded. Six policemen (policemen specifically) are attempting to use their bodies to get between the protestors and the windows. In response, the protestors sing louder. It feels dangerous. Residents in the local area have come out to see what's happening, and are shouting back at the protestors, not knowing or caring what is going on just wanting them to be quiet.

"What I think," says the woman with black hair. She'd said her name was... Joyce? That sounded right. "Is that the erasure of the term, 'woman', is a dangerous precedent. Once you erase something, its existence as a unique category ceases to exist, and that's why I'm here, really."

Ila wants to scream. Nobody here gets it. They don't get it at all. They don't get what is going to happen to them, to everyone, to young women all over the country. They had listened to her talk on the radio, some of the people here had even recognised her and nodded with approval, but they didn't understand. How could they?

She gets up to speak. The protest has gotten progressively louder, but the organisers have set up a microphone connected to an amp, so the speakers can be heard. She walks to the front of the room and holds the mic in her hand, shaking a little. The room stares at her. Faces upon faces, sitting, waiting expectantly.

"I'm Ila," she says.

Absurdly, for a moment it feels to her like some kind of addicts anonymous meeting. She half expects everyone to nod and reply, hello Ila, but they don't.

"I'm Ila, and three years ago I was raped by my best friend."

They're all quiet. The people outside might be loud and uncaring, but the ones in here were totally silent.

"She was, um. Well, I guess you wouldn't call her *she*, would you? I just always knew her as a she, and I never unlearned that, even after... okay, well. Let me get back to the start. I was raped by my best friend. We were trying to squat in this old house, on the edge of town. I don't even know why. It was a stupid thing. Stupid kids. You know."

She takes a deep breath, and, silently, apologises to Hannah for omitting her entirely. Hannah complicates things too much. Ila is telling the truth, everything she is saying is totally real to her, but to mention Hannah... it would overwhelm the story. Untether it from reality. She needs them to believe her. She needs them to know.

"So, we broke into this house. It had been empty for

decades and decades, we thought... I don't know, we were trying to prove some kind of point. We poked around, looking for secrets. Now, my friend, she was – and is, I guess – a trans-woman. A... trans-identified-male. Whatever you want to say, she's that. I'd always supported her in everything she did. I loved her so, so much, just. We were the closest two people have ever been. It's hard to explain how close, now, given what happened. But at the time it was, well, we came as a set. If you wanted one of us, you had to also have the other."

A chuckle, to herself. She is rambling, letting the story get out in front of her.

"We were in this old house, and as we explored, we found a room, down the... it's hard to describe. She found this room, and she lured me into it. I think she must have drugged me. I couldn't move. She raped me, so hard I thought I was going to die. And then. Then she..."

Ila feels tears welling up. She hadn't expected to really cry but trying to explain this to everyone in this room, with the shouting outside banging against the inside of her head, it's overwhelming her emotionally. Her fingers start to toy with the bottom of her shirt. Then, she lifts it up, just a little. Just enough to show her midriff.

It was difficult for her to explain to sexual partners that she had a Jewish mother and a Pakistani father and that she never, not in a million years, would she have done this to herself. Self-harm had been her friend during teenagerhood, and then again in the first year or two after the events at the House, when Ila had regressed, in many ways, to the coping mechanisms she had indulged in as an eighteen-year-old. But she hadn't done this. This hadn't been there before they went into that fucking room. It was there afterwards. She saw, in her mind's eye, Alice, standing over her with a blade in her hand. Bending down. Ila immobile on the floor. Bathed in red. Alice using the blade on her to make... to carve... in white, messy lines on the flesh between Ila's belly button and her vulva, words had been carved: ARBEIT MACHT FREI. Work will set you free. She had ancestors who had died there, in the slow, choking, grim forever of that camp, and ever since the House it had been on her body, a constant reminder. She hadn't gone to the police. How could she have gotten the police to arrest the only person she'd ever truly loved? But. Jesus.

Alice said that Ila raped her. Alice, too, had nightmarish memories. A scar to show for her time in the room. Ila didn't like to consider that. The possibility that, just maybe, she'd done something too. Or even worse, that her memory was false, and there was something even more horrific beneath.

She drops the shirt down, covering up the words again, to stop everyone gawking at her more than they already are. There had been a hope that sharing the story in full graphic detail to such a large number of people might have been liberating in some way, but it isn't. She just aches all over, and needs to sit down, which she does, slumped into her chair. Eyes from every corner of the room stare at her. Peeling away her clothes and her skin and her muscles and her bones.

After Alice and Ila had escaped the House, leaving whatever was left of Hannah there, Ila found herself slumped outside her parents' front door. She lay there for at least an hour before her father found her. Horrified, he carried her inside carefully and laid her upon her bed. She was only semi-conscious, her eyes half shut, her mouth making shapes but unable to properly form words. Ila's parents didn't know if they should call an ambulance, let her rest, or try to feed her. They couldn't see the wound on her stomach, which wasn't deep, but which was still wet and ripe. After agonising about the right course of action, they let her rest, whilst her mother made soup downstairs, trying her best to not sob into the saucepan. Ila woke up in her childhood bed, still dressed in the same clothes she had been wearing in the House, which were tattered and worn like they had been ravaged by some force. She felt like she was in a dream. A beautiful, simple dream. One which smelled like her mother's cooking, that aroma of particular ingredients wafting around her, nestling into her. She slipped out from underneath the sheets and padded, quietly, to the bathroom, leaning against the walls to make sure she didn't fall. Her feet were unsteady. Downstairs she could hear her mum choking back tears, trying to ask her dad what they should do, and her dad, his voice filled with a quiet, masculine terror, insisting that they needed to let her rest. They needed to ask her what had happened. Ila stopped, and went back into her room. She quietly lifted her mattress and found what she was looking for – a pair of scissors that had been there since she was a teenager. They'd never found it, not when they thought they had taken every sharp object she had. These were her secret. Age had not dulled them. She walked back to the bathroom and locked the door.

Her dad had to kick the door in. He found her in the empty bath, covered in blood, the scissors had dropped to the bathroom floor. That was what had alerted them that something was wrong. The noise of the scissors hitting the tiles. Her mother began to slowly repeat no, no, no, no, no, wringing her hands, no, no, no, God no not this. Her dad called an ambulance, and later the doctor said if they had been a minute slower, Ila would have died. As it was, she spent a week slipping in and out of consciousness. She dreamt of walls. Whenever she came to, she would grab the arm of whoever was at her bedside (if there was anybody there) and try to speak to them, but whatever she was trying to say was completely unintelligible, it simply came out as babbling and spit-flecked, like a baby trying to imitate the radio. She remained a high-risk patient for a month. She told the doctors that she had been raped. Her mum asked her who had raped her, but she said she couldn't remember. The painkillers made everything seem fluid, the world was smeared all over with Vaseline. The room she was in was white. The sun shone in through the window and made a yellow box in the middle of the floor. In the years since this moment, Ila would relapse, of course she would, but it is important to know that then, looking at the yellow patch of sun on the vinyl flooring of the hospital room, she decided that she would do her best to live.

The pub is a short while from where the meeting was held, and Ila is settling back with more wine, her nerves feeling calmed. The woman with the spiky black hair – Joyce – had bought it for her, and hugged her. "You were astoundingly brave," she told her. All Ila could do was shrug. "It was just what happened."

There were a couple of the people from the meeting here, sitting loosely in one corner of the pub. It wasn't an official continuation or anything, just a casual debrief, in Joyce's words. Joyce had a string of impressive credentials to her name, articles in all manner of newspapers and publications like the *Guardian* and the *New Statesman*. She was wearing a red suit with a black shirt and had bright orange frames for her glasses that made her look more eccentric than she really was. She had a precise, considered way of talking, and, drinking wine that Joyce had bought for her, Ila felt suddenly warm under her attentive, genuine gaze. The woman didn't seem interested in chatting to the others. Her focus was on Ila, and it made her blush, just a little bit, to have this older woman pay serious consideration to the things she thought and said.

"So, Ila," says Joyce. There was a particular way that she pronounced Ila's name, *ee-la*, that was technically incorrect, but she couldn't be bothered to properly correct it. "I heard you, you know. On the radio. I thought you were very astute. And then, today, you were passionate, a real burning ball of fury. Wonderful, both times. But I was wondering what you do when you aren't... you know... doing all of this?" She gestures at nothing, but Ila knows that she meant the wider debate, the TERF war, whatever you wanted to call it.

"I'm not so sure I do anything, really. I don't have a career. I have a little flat, and, well, I'll admit that my parents pay most of my rent for me." She felt embarrassed, admitting to that. "Sometimes I write freelance articles, and that brings in a bit, but nothing much."

"But what are your passions?" Joyce asks, leaning forwards.

Ila considers the question. "Well, books. I love books. I have a degree in literature, but I haven't, like, done anything with it. I've pitched reviews to some publications, but they never seem to want me."

"What books?" The woman was swigging at her wine like it was water.

"I love, um, this trend recently of feminist reworkings of fairy tales. Okay I know it's not a recent trend, I know Carter did it ages ago, but there's been an uptick in it recently. I found it fascinating, taking these patriarchal things that we ingrain into the minds of every little girl alive, and twisting them around."

Joyce looked excited. There was a childlike glee in her green eyes. Ila wanted to make her happy. Joyce asked if Ila had read this or that book, the book with that story with the woman growing strange teeth, the one with the story about the women unravelling. Ila had read both.

"She's one of us," Joyce says with a conspiratorial grin,

referring to one of the authors she mentioned, and Ila wasn't sure if she had meant that the author was gender critical or a lesbian, or, possibly, both.

"Excuse me," says Ila. "I, um, have to pee."

Joyce chuckles. "Go ahead, go ahead," she says, waving her hands in the general direction of the women's toilets.

Ila had been worrying, just a little, that some of the TRAs, the trans activists that had been protesting earlier, might come to this pub. But none of them seemed to be here. She, of course, didn't know this, but the reason was that Gemma hadn't found out which pub they were going to. Gemma had gone off to join the protestors at a bar, brimming with anxious energy after the day she'd had.

Ila went into the toilets and found that the floor was a little wet. Her footsteps made gross splashes as she walked towards a decaying stall, nothing like the space age ones at the meeting earlier, and emptied her bladder slightly clumsily. How much had she drunk? When she came out of the stall, Joyce was there, between her and the sinks.

"Hi," slurs Ila.

"You're very pretty," says Joyce. "Just, a startlingly pretty young woman. I couldn't believe what that man did to you." It felt weird to hear Alice be called a man, even if Ila thought that she was.

"Um. Could I wash my hands?" she asks.

Instead of moving out of the way, Joyce steps forwards, backing her into the stall she had just been in. The woman was faster than she seemed capable of. Two steps, and there she was, her body pressed against Ila's, and Ila clumsily went backwards, banging the insides of her knees into the rim of the toilet and crashing down so she was sitting on it again. Joyce stands over her, and gently but firmly, spreads Ila's legs apart. Ila can't look at her face.

"Please stop that," she mumbles.

"I'm so happy that we met," says the woman, her strong perfume mixing with the smell of shit from the stall next to this one.

Ila wants to screw her eyes shut as tight as she possibly can, so tight that it hurts, she wants to do that and find that when she opens them again the woman isn't there at all, that she has never been there. But she shuts her eyes, and she can still feel Joyce's hand moving up one of her thighs, unbuttoning her jeans. Ila's body goes limp.

"I think," she's forcing out the words, using all of her strength, "that you should leave, now." There's no affect in Ila's voice. It was almost too much to even speak.

"Why?" asks Joyce, sounding genuinely hurt.

Ila opens her eyes. She can see the woman now, silhouetted in the light. No. This isn't going to happen. The woman steps back, out of the stall, looking at Ila with confusion.

"You can't tell anyone," says Joyce.

Ila pushes her palms against the walls of the toilet stall and heaves herself up. Her jeans are still undone, and hang, loosely, around her thighs. "Why not?" Ila asks. Strength is easing its way back into her.

"I'm too important to this movement."

"I don't care." Ila is burning with rage.

"You know what it would do, if someone came out and said a prominent... one of us..."

"I don't care."

"Think, for a second, Ila. I'm trying to be reasonable here!" She must be worried about someone else walking in here. It could happen at any moment. "Think about it. Think about what happened to you. If you were to say anything, it could tank everything, put so many girls in the same position. Use your brain!"

And Ila does think. She thinks about what would happen if she tweeted about this, or posted about it on a blog. Either all the others would gang up on her, accuse her of lying, being a secret transactivist, or... if people did believe her. What then? Joyce nodded. She could see what had gone through Ila's head. She turns and leaves. Joyce's footsteps on the wet floor walk away, back to the warm friendly lights of the pub. For fuck's sake, Ila says to herself, standing there with her jeans falling down her legs. For fuck's sake.

HOUSE

The House has been waiting for so long. A square blotch of darkness against the landscape, like a townhouse but sitting alone, lonely with its back to the trees. The House was once a pale limestone, but over the years it has blackened. The House sits a little way back from the main road, but choking fumes from the exhaust pipes of passing trucks settle on the House's skin. The House doesn't like this. *Filth,* it thinks. *Disgusting filth all over my body no one to wash me but the rains no one to wash me but the rains yet a storm will come and cleanse me surely.* The House's front faces that busy road and, over the other side, a tower block, jutting upwards, tall enough that its shadow is cast over the House's face. All the House can look at is this; the modern world, and it despises what it sees. Its back is to the forest, the trees encircle it and then stretch out up the hill behind it, growing thick and deep and dangerous. Thirty years ago, a man, not from here, snatched a young girl who was walking home from school. He locked her into his van, and kept her there for a week, before dragging her out beneath the trees. He butchered her there. Then, after doing what he did, he buried her beneath the largest tree, like an offering. The man will die in prison. He will rot.

There had been a train station, once, where the tower block now stands. Thatcher's government gutted the trains, and many of the stations faded away, the land they were built on sold off to men in dark suits waiting in the wings for the right time to build, and profit. Some nights, some of the people who live in that tower block walk, without knowing why, to their windows and look down, across the black expanse of the night, across the busy street, towards the House. They stand at their windows, their breath fogging up the glass. If you asked them what they were looking for, or why, none of them would have a clue.

The House looks back up at them. *I'm still here. I'm still here. You can see me.*

A man named Jeremy was trying to recover from addiction. He lived, alone, in social housing, in a depressing flat in that exact block. But, despite the sometimes-grim environment, he was doing well. Narcotic's Anonymous had helped him work through everything immensely. In fact, he hadn't touched the drugs in half a year, and now, with the help of a local housing charity, he had been able to secure this flat. A place to live, safely. He found work at a little cafe that sold vegan food. Jeremy wasn't vegan when he started there but, after being there a month, he felt like he would never touch meat again. A routine grew organically around him. He went to work, he came home, he watched TV, ate simple meals, slept. This was the cycle of his life. He hoped to take up a hobby soon. Perhaps, he thought, I might start birdwatching. Birds had always made him happy.

On the evening of December 3rd, 1998, he walked, without thinking, to the window that looked down from his flat, across the dark expanse of the road, towards the House. It wasn't visible tonight. There was a thick fog in the air. When cars and trucks shot passed, down the road, their headlights looked like the eyes of ghosts.

He felt drunk, although he had not had any alcohol, not for over a year now. But the world rushed around him. There was a stairwell beneath his feet, his footsteps heavy. Then the cold air, the fog all around, cloaking the streetlights, cloaking everything, wet and cold on his skin. He stumbled forwards, in the direction of the House. *Come to me.* He couldn't hear it, of course. It had no real voice. But still. It sat there, in the dark on the other side of the road, calling for him. He was so confused and so intent on trying to get to the House, that he never saw the National Express coach which ploughed straight into him as he tried to cross the road, leaving a wet, bloody mangled mess behind it that looked nothing at all like Jeremy. They had to wash him off of the street.

That block of flats has the highest-percentage death rate of any block in the city. Nobody knows this, or, if they do, they are not the sort of person to care. Pets go missing from the flats there more than anywhere else, especially cats. The cats... it was inexplicable. They'll be there one day, mewing and beloved, but the next they're gone, with no clear sign of where they went.

Cats vanish. It's a simple fact. Something that everybody who owns one has to deal with, sooner or later. Not every cat, of course. But cats, in general, are not like dogs, they don't stay at your side loyally. They vanish. They have secret lives that you will never know about. Somebody a few flats over might say they thought they saw the cat heading towards the House, over the road, and the owner is anxious that the cat was run over, just like that man, Jeremy, had been only the other week, but they can't find any evidence of that. However much they love their cat, they do not look for it in the House. Sometimes, the House wants them to. But, if they are in their right mind, they do not follow the trail of breadcrumbs that leads through its broken doorway and up its dark stairs into its throat which is crimson and wet, dripping with decay. No, if the cat went to the House then it will never be seen again. That is a fact of life for those that live here. The owners can hope and pray that instead, it might have run into the forest, to live on a diet of field mice and shrews, but who can say, really.

There are a number of unexplained suicides in the flats. People killing themselves, without ever having shown signs of mental illness previously. Of course, people do not have to show symptoms to be struggling, but... don't you think it's strange that all these working-class people, single mums, second generation immigrants, will walk to their windows, and look down at the House, a splintered but welcoming visage, the House looking up at them, wormwood eating through its guts.... don't you think it's strange that they all decide, then and there, to take their own lives?

Haunted houses are rarely neat. If the House was truly haunted, then that haunting spilled out of its broken or boarded up windows, soaking into the fertile earth around it. The trees still grow, but the squirrels in their branches often feel the sudden need to bite each other in the eyes. Even if the cats from the block of flats made it safely into the trees, they may not be safe. But despite all of this, people still choose to live in those flats. They still hike in the woods. There are some who immediately feel safer, knowing that the House is there, and there are some who do not. For someone to be comfortable, another has to be uncomfortable. For someone to feel safe, another has to be unsafe. And the one who is safe may not even be safe, they may just *feel* safe, up until the moment they don't. For someone, the majority, to prosper, another has to... well. I think you understand what I am saying, and why. For a house to be built another has to be knocked down, converted, the occupants flushed out into the wilderness with nothing to hold on to.

For one live organism to continue to exist, another live organism must stop existing all together.

The House sat, waiting for its girls.

ALICE

Last night I dreamt I went to work again. Lying on the bathroom floor I fell asleep, my head ripe and throbbing with pain. I remember falling to the floor, my head resting on a towel. The lights were still on above me. Then I was gone. In the recesses of unconsciousness, I dreamt I went to work again.

Again? I don't work. Not really. I don't really have a job. Sometimes, men give me money to watch me do things around the flat, cleaning, dressing, eating, that sort of thing. Sex work is work, I guess, but I don't know if what I do is really even sex work. The other day I tried to clean my flat, which is work, and I set up my laptop's webcam to look at me while I did it. I've done this before, many times. I'm always shocked when I look back at the grainy video. The way my body moves is weird. I don't know if it moves differently because I know there's a camera there... maybe I always have that particular fake feminine sway to my hip, or maybe I'm putting it on.

The other thing men pay for is me talking to the camera, brainwashing them. "Look at me," I say, focusing on my lips, dry and cracked but in the pixelated image they look deep red and ripe. "Look at me. Are you ready? I want you to imagine that you are out, after dark, in the deep neon pink lights of a gay club. Now, I know, I know. You're not gay, are you? You're not a faggot. I know that. You've told me many times, that you aren't gay." When they pay me, the men will send me what they need from the video. A lot of the time they go to great lengths to explain that no, they're not gay, they're not trans either. They just. They just need this, okay? "You aren't gay. You came to the gay club because you're comfortable in your masculinity. You don't mind if a muscular gay man hits on you, do you? Because you know you aren't gay. You know you like tits. You love to hold tits in your hands, put them in your mouth, suck on the sensitive nipples. But you were okay there, in the gay club. It's just that straight men are programmed to be a little on edge around gay men. That's all. You aren't homophobic, right?"

I take a long drink of water, and light up a cigarette. The smoke in the low-quality playback blurs my face.

"Boobs are amazing, aren't they? Just touching them. Just thinking about them. I know. You can't hide it from me. Sure, you're a straight man. But you think about what it would be like to have boobs, don't you? You daydream about lying in bed and holding your chest firmly in two cupped hands. That's okay. A lot of *men* do that... a lot of *men* dream about slipping their fingers between their thighs and finding a soft wet cunt there." I lean in close to the camera so the only thing visible is my lips. "You want to suck dick, don't you? When you were in that gay club you wanted to go into the back room with the biggest man there, the biggest..." I can feel myself hesitating. "Take the biggest, blackest cock in your mouth."

The *black cock* thing is... uncomfortable. I know that. But if they ask for it, when they send me money for the video, I make sure to include it. I'm not in a position to say no.

"You're a fucking sissy," I say, "and the only way for you to be a woman is if you suck a cock, is if you bend over and take it in your little pussy, whimpering like an animal, squealing like a pig."

I get up off the bathroom floor feeling gravity right itself around me. I walk, tentatively, into my bedroom and crawl into my bed. In the poster opposite, the singer's mouth is open, stuck forever in the middle of telling a racist joke. His eyes would be moving in their sockets if he still had them.

I love the smell of bleach. I sometimes wonder if I am a bad girl because I am not particularly clean. I don't mean 'bad girl' in the way that I am a bad girl whilst I get fucked, I mean that I wonder if I am... insufficient. My mother told me once, with genuine confusion, that I used to be much neater before I came out to her ("before you were a girl"), and now that I am out ("now that you are a girl") I am a mess, and that this is not how it should be, because girls should be clean. And when I clean, on video, I look like a man, I look like a man doing a bad impression of a French maid, or something like that. I look like a drag parody. But whatever, it makes me that extra twenty pounds, and I can spend that money on weed, or on a cheap bottle of vodka, or maybe even on food. But still. I look like a man, and I try not to watch the videos. Gender is as much about the air around you, the kind of place you are in, as how you look and how you act. And how you feel inside barely means anything at all, in the grand scheme of things.

In the House, Hannah looked beautiful in the torchlight.

She didn't look it, but she loved metal, and she always found herself the object of the affection of pagan-seeming men with huge beards and runic tattoos, because she was small, white and blonde. She never reciprocated that affection of course. She fell into the orbit of Ila and I, became our third wheel, in a way, although Ila and I never actually dated. We met at university and were grouped together by a bored seminar tutor who was filling out his work hours to try and get back to his PhD. By that point, Ila and I had already met. We went for coffee practically every day, and I talked about Heidegger, and the flaws of his view of existentialism. To that, Ila would poke me in the ribs, and tell me I missed out the fact that he was a Nazi, that was a pretty big flaw, all told, and I would roll my eyes. Hannah was a strange addition to this equation. I'm not sure she could have even told you who Heidegger was, let alone what he had said or done. But pretty soon it was always us three, we would sit and drink rum, listen to Burzum, which Ila would say made her uncomfortable, but when we were drunk enough the three of us would be jumping around the room and screaming, and Ila, despite her brown skin, would joke about the purity of white women, her eyes on Hannah. I did that too. I'll admit that. I wouldn't do that now, of course. I crawl from bed again to make a black coffee. I'm supposed to be filming some sissy hypno today, but the thought of that makes me wobble on my feet. I go back to bed, holding the steaming mug in one hand, trying not to spill it on my sheets.

When I was younger, I used to use 4chan, and I would post pictures of my face, asking if I passed as a girl. *no you don't you look like a man with that jawline you will never* and on and on, that was the response, and I would respond similarly in turn when others, the same people who had said that, posted pictures of themselves, desperately trying to look like girls from various anime, angling the camera so it made their eyes big, white, shiny, sticking out their tongues. I posted stark black and white pictures of me, with my thick black glasses and my long hair. *ur hair doesn't look like a girls hair it looks like a mans hair which has grown long.* The window for passing, according to 4chan, is between twenty and twenty-five, so I'm edging into *hon* territory now. Pictures of white trans girls aged seventeen with pink wigs pulled down over their faces making peace signs, and in the background, hanging on their wall, a red flag with a white circle in the middle and two black lightning bolts. Or their fursonas, dogs with tongues lolling out, dressed in sexy SS-uniforms, but with space for a human cleavage. *anyone ever notice how trans tits look like dog tits lol.* If you scrolled down the board you realised that almost every girl on there was white. The ones who said they were Japanese never seemed to post pictures, so everyone assumed that they were also white, and just lying because they wished they were Japanese. I never did any of this, of course, I never had a fursona, and I definitely never posed with Nazi flags. But I still look at those places sometimes. I still press my head into the corners of the internet. Sometimes I look for clients there, sometimes I look for things that will make my skin crawl. On a fetish forum I wouldn't be able to find again, I came across a long, repetitive string of German words when looking for people with sissy fetishes. The person who posted it had no personal information on their profile, and this was, as far as I could tell, their only post on the site. The translation is probably somewhat inaccurate, because I only used the automatic Google translation tool. But I don't think it was exactly coherent anyway. And when I read it, I felt – I became sure – that the author was addressing me and me alone.

Ohhhhhhhhh yesssss she looks so hot and sexy in a latex mini dress and knee-high black fuck me boots Can't stand how awesome she looks hmmmm? xD xD xD xD You can't do anything and that will make you ugly shitty transvestite pig glow hahahahah. You will have to endure forever how awesome she looks. And do you know what you goddamn shit tranny pig? She would surely lift her sexy latex maid slut apron dress and grill your useless eggs and your mini cock and digested it into your throat before slowly and painfully squeezing you out of the messy stuffing pile of toddlers with slippery household garbage bags and neat bulky waste. Betting? Ohhhhhhh she looks sooooooo sexy mhhhhhh? In contrast to you completely crazy women wearing transvestite pig shit. Buaaaaa. God hates transvestite pigs. God Loves Latex Maid Babes. God loves Latex Nazi she-wolf Babes. The latex maid celebrity babe TV show - in the garbage truck, you shit transvestite pig. Shit transvestite pigs as Latex Maid Bitch just cheeky laughing and latex Maid apron fluttering together with slippery household garbage bags, full of food scraps and fully pooped baby diapers and puffed bulky waste, hissing, squeezing and squeezing dead and compressing and incinerating in the waste incineration plant, only to be celebrated and fucked all night long as a national heroine latex maid apron If you still urge us on your ridiculous perversion to bother the publicity in women's clothes, they will be eliminated as much as you deserve them, and you will simply be put together with slippery household garbage bags then crushed and burned in the garbage incineration plant. Because: Does God like it when transvestites wear our sexy latex dresses and thus unashamedly destroy the tension between man and woman? No. He certainly doesn't like that. God loves Latex Maid Bitches and Latex Maid Bitches don't like shitty transvestites. That's why God now allows the Latex Maid TV Show - Into the garbage truck, you shitty transvestite pig. Because feminism is the annihilation of the misguided woman (transvestite pig) by the well-advised (latex maid babe). A mega hot live reality TV show moderated by latex celebrities, in which every time three other sexy girls in latex maid mini dresses slip on and grin latex maid flap aprons, pull black hold-up seamed nylons over the thighs, high-gloss polyester satin women neckerchiefs, Dressed like this, they can tear the shaggy transvestite's clothes off a shit pig and put on really embarrassing yellow rubber pants and then beat up the shit shit pig and meet. After that, the booted latex maid sluts throw the shitty clothes carrier naked, only with the buttoned rubber pants, into a huge black, half-full plastic garbage can and throw the freak-wearing miscarriage with slippery household garbage bags, which are filled with lukewarm mad food scraps and fully-packed baby diapers. The latex dress cheers and screams: At the climax of the show, the latex maid sluts pour the shitty fickdreck transvestite pig together with household waste into the household waste incineration plant in order to shred and burn it. The latex maid girls toast with champagne in front of the household waste incineration chamber, while the shitty transvestite pig waste smokes from the chimney and is burned to useful heat energy, with which the latex maid bitch polishes her French nails provocatively and visibly amused. The only use of a fucking transvestite pig! Just as God would have wanted, because God loves latex maid bitch and latex maid bitch hate shitty transvestite pig. Especially women wearing latex dresses wearing shit garments. The time comes when transvestism is declared sick and dangerous. In this show, which only women / girls from 18 years of age are allowed to attend in sexy latex dress outfits. Three particularly sexy looking, big-breasted girls, whose age is a maximum of 26 years, can apply for the show, as an active latex maid babe, to squeeze a shitty transvestite sweat together with slippery, jam-packed household garbage bags in a garbage truck with thunderous applause and then in to incinerate the household waste incineration plant. In addition, girls can apply *for this show as an active latex maid who can show that they personally know the shitty transvestite pig who has been released for the removal of the goddamned woman's clothes, and it would therefore be a real treat for them if they threw this anti-socialist offense. In addition, this girl has to convince the jury how sadistic and lousy she will make the well-known shitty transvestite pig suffer before she, along with two other sexy latex maid babes, along with masses of household garbage bags, filled with slippery food scraps and fully pooped baby diapers and one thrown over it Leaves leather couch in the huge latex maid babe garbage truck with a loud laugh Splashing and cracking*

When I read it, I couldn't help imagining myself stuck in this pervert's fantasy. And the woman torturing me, pressing her heels down on my face.

I could go back to sleep. I could do nothing but sleep. I could lie here all day until my body becomes one with the filthy bedsheets like John and Yoko, only not even leaving to shit. The outside world doesn't always seem possible. I could stay here beneath your eyes, Mr. Poster. Would you like that?

I screw my eyes shut and think of the dream, so it doesn't fade away from me. Still lying there prone on the towel, I dream that I go down a steep set of stairs into a freezing underground station. The stairs go on for some time. When I get to the bottom, I turn down a short tunnel which opens out into the station, which is cavernous but flooded and overfull.

They are packed tightly in. The bodies. The poor, the sick, the needy. They have vermin crawling over them. Amongst this mass of faceless poverty, I see an old friend from university. He says that he starts working at the factory today. What factory? He shrugs and I remember, oh yes, of course, I am also starting work at the factory. Down on the train tracks, where water pools, sparks begin to shoot up, violent flashes of light. The train is coming. Everything smells like piss. I see things floating through water on the tracks, and I try to look closer but now the train is pulling up and the crowd is pulling me onto it, charmless great ugly masses desperate to toil.

In dreams, as in life, I don't remember the section of this experience that is a journey. It doesn't really register at all. I'm there, pressed into the writhing mass of workers on the train, and now I am in the factory, free of the crowd, standing in front of countless gates. I do not know where I have to go. Nobody's told me. I must be told what to do. *Look here now. This is what you are going to do.* Everybody is going somewhere. There are wires carrying blue light up above me, and, in the distance, a tower. I head towards it, because that seems like the sort of place where I should be working.

Because this is a dream, everything looks like it was shot on a black and white super-8 camera, with sound recorded in post-production and colour lightly painted onto the frames.

I'm now inside the tower, looking at stone steps winding up the inside of it. These are markedly different stone steps to the ones leading down into the underground station. We have moved, aesthetically, from post-industrial dystopia to the Gothic, with maybe a hint of steampunk. I am now at work. My job is to climb the stairs, to circle up the insides of this great gothic phallus. In the dream I acknowledge that I know this is a phallus.

The stairs wind up between distinct levels, with floors but no furniture. On each of these levels there is an open window, no glass, not even a frame. At every window stands a person. They have their backs to me. On one of the levels, I call to the person standing there – a woman, I think – but she doesn't respond at all.

You're thinking, how is this a factory? Which I suppose is understandable. A factory is, among other things, an aesthetic concept, one that we can all get immediately, even if we have never been to a real factory ourselves. Factories are about men working, operating machines, hard hats, that old silent film of the workers leaving at the end of their shift, choked lungs and calloused hands. But more than anything I suppose what a 'factory' is, is a hub of production. I know this tower is a factory, or part of one. But I don't know what it produces. It must produce something, or it wouldn't be a factory, and I know it is a factory, so it has to produce something. After a few more levels, there stops being people at the windows. I am alone now. Or maybe I'm not. Maybe I just hope that I am.

The further up the tower I walk, I become aware of it. Something is following. I can't hear it, I do not know what it is. But I know it's there, that it is climbing the tower behind me, matching my pace, always a floor or so behind me. I have to keep going up. What happens when I reach the top? Will I be out of a job? Will they carry my limp, broken body to the Jobcentre? Will they declare me fit to work? I start to climb faster. I'm trying, very hard, not to look over my shoulder. This tower/factory is haunted, like all workplaces, haunted by the people who have done these same mechanical actions, made the same mechanical statements, cried in the disabled toilets in the middle of every shift, haunted by the feet of every person who has climbed this tower before I have, trying, desperately, not to look over their shoulder, but knowing that there is no escape because the tower doesn't go on forever and it doesn't lead to anywhere else. One of these floors will be the last. I can't tell which. When I reach the top I will have nowhere to go but... down? Down the outside? Is this what the jumpers felt on 9/11? Not that I'm trying to, I don't know, steal valour from the 9/11 jumpers, I am just panicking at this point, trying to force myself awake. How do I even know there is something behind me? I cannot prove that it is there. As I said, I can't hear it, I'm refusing to look. Can I smell it? I can smell dust, and nothing else. So, I can't prove that it is there, yet I am convinced. If it reaches me something so horrible will happen that it is preferable that I die.

I turn to my right, to see a window. Outside, the world is a great white expanse. I climb up, clumsily, onto the window ledge. I peer up out and see that above me, the tower stretches up still further, but I can see its point. And below me, I can see the ground. I can see a garden of beautiful flowers. If I jump, my body will fall into that garden and decay. I will be eaten apart by worms and little insects. I will be fertiliser. And at the last moment, as I prepare myself, in the dream, to jump, I look behind me. The dream changes perspective. I see my own face, looking over my shoulder. My eyes thick with tears and my mouth open. My face is reacting to seeing something that I can't see. My mouth opens even in a silent scream. Then I am gone. I fall. I jump. Last night I dreamt I went to work again. Last night I dreamt of suicide, again. It seemed to me I stood a while at the moment beforehand, and I could not enter, I could not fall, not until suddenly I could. Then, like all dreamers, I was possessed all of a sudden with supernatural powers, and I passed like a spirit through the barrier before me.

Then like all dreamers I was possessed. And passed like a spirit.

Then I was possessed.

And now I'm awake, feeling like shit. A pain throbs in my head. The flat is freezing cold. Last night, I left the window open.

I had a plant once, which became infested with little larvae, which turned into little flies. They covered my flat's walls, fucking, and laying eggs in my food. I screamed because I didn't know what to do, and my neighbours complained to the agency. This was in my old flat. When I moved, I promised myself that I would do better this time around, with this flat. I would try to clean it once a week on average, I would open up the windows and the curtains to let air and light into my space, to stop myself from turning into the worst version of myself, sick like something that has lived in a cave all of its life, sick and gasping. And maybe if I kept the place neat, then the ghosts would feel less comfortable haunting me. I don't know if ghosts thrive in squalor. The most famous haunted places in the world tend to be the big houses and castles, because rich people lived in them and the collective blood on their hands, the collective violence that they caused on everybody else in the world, manifests into ghosts.

Ghosts are born from trauma and violence.

I pull myself from the daze I was in beneath the bedsheets, forcing myself upwards. I make coffee. I hustle or whatever. Glancing in the mirror, last night's eyeliner smeared down my cheeks, skin pale and sickly like fog. Girlboss. Wash your face clean, brush the knots from your hair, eyes watering as you tear through each tangle. Change into a new dress. Put more makeup on then maybe you won't be so fucking corpselike. Open your laptop. I open my laptop and look at the pixelated face that stares back at me captured by the webcam. Fuck you, I tell it. Fuck you, it says back to me. A man sent me money for a video, but I haven't been able to think about making it. I saw his specific instructions and I couldn't look at them. But I still took the money, didn't I? Not too proud to refuse money on ethical or moral grounds. I look at the instructions again. I think about them. I vocalise them.

"I know how you used to sneak into your mother's chest of drawers and pull out her panties and rub them all over your little sissy body, before putting them on. I know how you would wear her make-up and her high heels when she was out, and watch yourself, in the mirror, strutting about. You've never told anyone about that, have you? But I know. I know everything about you. I can see into your soul. I can see every dark corner you have. You don't live at home anymore but at Christmas when you go back to visit you tease yourself with the thought. You still want to wear Mummy's panties, don't you? You are worthless. Worthless little sissy boy dreaming of being a girl." I'm shaking, and I don't know if you can tell in the video. "If you want to be a girl then act like it. Go on. Bend over, and take a big dick deep in your pussy. Let it stretch you out until you barely exist, until the big dick is the thing that defines you, until it fills up every single inch of your insides. Whimper. Go on. Whimper, little sissy pig. If you don't have a big black cock with you, then use something else, use a dildo. You like your dildo don't you? Let it fuck you. Scream like a hysterical little girl as it fucks you. Like a hysterical little girl getting…"

I say what he wants me to say, but automatically. I don't think the words. They just happen, they come out of my mouth, and the shame and the disgust wash over me until I can't take it anymore. I turn off the video. There are some sick people out there.

I look at my phone, and see that Jon's texted, asking for updates about what happened with Sabi. *Did you fuck her then?* When I slept, I dreamt of work. She wasn't in the dream at all. In fact, her absence was notable. There was a space somewhere in the centre of the dream that she was supposed to fill, but somebody had pulled her out of it, roughly, leaving a gaping wound. Perhaps she was what was following me, that unseen horror. But that thing could just as well have been something else, some other nightmare from my trauma following me. Hannah, maybe, twisting, clawing after me. Or five older boys circling me, when I was, oh, I must have been nine. One of them told me he had seen my mum's tits. Which honestly, I just found strange, because he had never met my mum. These boys took me into the forest. The floor was covered in wet mud, mud so wet it would have been possible to sink into it. There was a wooden plank suspended from a tree, with a rusted nail poking out the underside of it. The boys, I can't remember their faces, they all look the same in this memory, told me to stand underneath the rusted nail. If I would do that, then I could join their gang. I knew that if I did this, they would make the plank drop from the tree, which would send the rusted nail into the top of my skull, killing me. And inside the rusted nail, a woman was being chased by another woman, they were looking for work, they thought they were going upwards, ascending, but their centre of gravity was all wrong. In fact, they were headed down. But they never made it, they never found fulfilling or honest work, they just simply kept climbing until one or both of them was dead. Climbing a tower is unskilled work. Cleaning is also unskilled work. Filming yourself making sissy hypno is unskilled labour. Climbing a tower, being chased by an unseen entity which might be the woman who raped you when you were in a haunted house, is not an easy job, and it seems unfair to describe it as unskilled, considering there are a lot of factors which go into it, certainly not everybody could do that job. For one, you have to be physically fit enough to climb all those stairs. Of course, outside of my unconscious, I am probably not fit enough to do this, but inside it was a possibility. You have to be able to do that. You have to have been raped by a woman inside a haunted house. It's not clear if the scar you have in the shape of a cunt on your forehead is required for the job, but I suspect it might be. Furthermore, not everybody can work in such a haunted place, in such a place steeped in obvious, rusting, decaying symbolism as this tower, or this house, or my flat, in fact, with cracks in the walls, with a carpet thick with dirt that is impossible to clean, with the eyeless gaze of the man in the poster, did I even hang the poster back up or did it hang itself?, its eyeless gaze always looking at you wherever you fucking turn, and the lone eye of your webcam watching you as well, and who knows who is watching through the window, through the cracks in the ceiling, through every little gap. I think the room has to find something to look through. When I took away the singer's eyes, it had to search for new eyes. There were no real eyes left, so it had to spread itself thin and use other, more abstract things to represent eyes. It had to watch me, it had to see and laugh and call me a degenerate or a fag or whatever it wanted to call me, whilst still wanting to be inside of me or for me to be inside of it. And of course, it being a room, I am inside of it. And it is inside of me.

Has the man in the poster ever tried to fuck me? If he

could see me then there would have at least been an attempt. But... it's like the end of Jane Eyre. Mr Rochester is blinded in the house fire, which means he no longer has power over Jane. The eyes are, in Freud, akin to the tesitcles, and him losing the eyes means he is castrated of masculinity. Jane looks after him. This eyeless ghost cannot and will not try to exert dominance over me. I know it is problematic for me, and for Freud, to use blindness here as a way of castrating men. It's an easy shorthand, and I don't think it is acceptable at all. I'm sure blind men are just as capable of violence as men who can see.

I open Ila's message. *We should talk.* Maybe she didn't mean to send it to me, although how she would accidentally have sent it is unclear. I don't want to speak to her. I had a therapist last year. We struggled to find the root of my trauma. He didn't believe me when I said I had been inside a haunted house, but he did believe that *something* had happened. I told him about the boys and their rusted nail, and I told him about how, months later, I found my father's toolbox. I selected a nail and dangled it over my head, but it wasn't the same. The nail was brand new, unblemished. It has to be rusted for it to work again.

"For *what* to work again? How did it feel, when those boys were doing that to you?"

"Doing what to me?"

"Touching you," he said.

"They didn't touch me," I replied.

Poor Sabi. The man in the poster can come for me all he

wants, but Sabi didn't deserve that. He grabbed at her. He tried to pull her down into the shadows under my bed.

If I tear the poster down and throw it out, the haunting won't be stopped. But, after last night, the thought of him coming out of it again, standing there above me, is too much. So, this time I actually do it. I pull it down, walk over to the open window, and drop it out into the air. The poster flutters down from the window of my flat. It drops low to the pavement and then is caught again by the wind and lifted up higher, looping through the air like a racist bird. A hand shoots up to catch it out of the air. A man pulls the poster down and looks at it. He smirks. Let's call this man Kasim. This is something you may not be aware of, but the band in the poster have always been very popular within the South Asian immigrant communities in the UK. This might be surprising, given the singer's frequent Islamophobic outbursts, but his feelings around Islam and immigration were not common knowledge at the height of their popularity. I suppose people often think that, back then, he wasn't racist at all. But that seems unlikely. The moment he started a solo career, he danced on stage with women wearing Union Jacks. What seems more accurate would be to say that he was not open about his beliefs back then. Perhaps he didn't even realise he had them. Bigotry can sit inside of you, hardening, turning into something painful before you even realise it is there. If you attend the meeting of a fascist political group, for example, you were not made fascist by that group, you were already a fascist, but one who did not have an outlet. Radicalisation is a complicated thing.

I think often what it actually does is simply nurture an idea that was already there, inside of you. His solo career gave him the space, and the platform, to begin to express these ideas, away from the influence of other band members. I do not know how his ideas were nurtured. But he did not wake up one day and decide to be racist. But his songs actually spoke to young South Asian boys in some interesting ways, which he clearly did not intend. Kasim was one of these boys. Although he was now grown up, he remembers listening to those songs in his bedroom when he felt confused about who he was, about the fact that he was attracted to the white skinhead boy who lived down the road who hated him. Kasim wonders who this poster belonged to, and why they crossed out the eyes. He knows the singer of the band has said some bad things recently, but the strange chance of this poster flying through the air and into his hand feels like fate, so he folds it up and puts it into his laptop bag. By the time he gets home, though, he has completely forgotten about it. He leaves it in his bag. He cooks his boyfriend dinner. They talk about their days, and his boyfriend asks if anything special happened, but Kasim says that no, nothing happened really, nothing at all. And that night, when his boyfriend goes to get a glass of water from the sink in the kitchen, the man in the poster crawls out of the poster, weaker, transparent, flickering and cold. He stands in the middle of the kitchen, behind Kasim's boyfriend. He has his back turned, filling up a glass from the tap over the kitchen sink. The singer tries to say something, but finds that not only is he eyeless, he is also now without the strength of a voice. Kasim's boyfriend turns, then, and sees him. He drops the glass, yelling with shock at the sight of the transparent singer standing in his kitchen. The singer fades out of view. Kasim runs down from the bedroom to ask what's wrong, but his boyfriend doesn't know what to say. I thought I saw a man, he mutters. But... he vanished.

God knows what the fucking looney left will destroy next.

I don't see it at first. I let the poster fall from the window and watch it go, fluttering away in the wind. Good riddance. I should have done that a long time ago. I only put you up to cover that mark on the wall.

The mark on the wall. I turn around to look at it, and there it is. Still present, but different now. Even since Sabi was here it's grown, without my knowledge, in only a day. Spreading. Infecting the wallpaper around it. I walk closer, but I know what it is. I have thought about that face so much, my mind racked with guilt. I'd know it anywhere.

The stain on the wall has spread, and in the stain is a face, with wide eyes in immense pain and a mouth open, silently screaming. Hannah's face. We went with her into the House, and she never came out. Now she's here. In my wall. Motionless. Looking right at me.

ILA

Sissy porn produces transwomen like a factory, a great industry which takes insecure men and pushes them through oil-slick machines until they fall out the other end, confused and clutching pink frilly panties to their chests. Ila has watched sissy porn before, out of perverse interest. She's seen a lot of it. Know how thy enemy thinks. She put a piece out on Medium about the ways in which it enforces sexist visions of femininity. *All of sissy porn*, she wrote, *is about trying to produce a particular kind of feminine ideal, one with huge breasts and a petite waist and big, anime eyes surrounded by long lashes. So much of it is about trying to convince the people consuming it – men – that if they want to be 'fucked by cock' then that means they're a woman, because a woman is only defined by her relationship to 'taking cock' in the mouth or vagina or rectum. That at the end of it all, the only thing a woman is, is a hole.* The piece closed with a quote from Dworkin, in her speech about prostitution: "I ask you to think about your own bodies – if you can do so outside the world that the pornographers have created in your minds, the flat, dead, floating mouths and vaginas and anuses of women [...] I ask you to think concretely about your own bodies used that way. How sexy is it? Is it fun? The people who defend prostitution and pornography want you to feel a kinky little thrill every time you think of something being stuck in a woman. I want you to feel the delicate tissues in her body that are being misused. I want you to feel what it feels like when it happens over and over and over and over and over and over and over again."

She thinks a lot about Joyce. In her memory of the event, which feels like it belongs to someone else, the moment Joyce stepped towards her, pushing into the stall, her face changed. In the image it twists to become Alice's face. Looking down at her. That fucking jawline, the ones she knows so well, that, when drunk, she would trace her index finger across, sharp enough that it could have cut her hand open. Alice was so much taller than her, tall like a tower, like a pillar holding up the earth. Too tall to be a woman but... those thick eyebrows that Alice always refused to wax. Alice's brown eyes, Alice's brown curly hair twisting at her shoulders. It's hard to even accept that it was the old woman instead, in that moment. Looking down at her, and her a piece of ripe fruit, plump and juicy and ready to be bitten.

She didn't know how Joyce got her email address, but, a few days after the bathroom incident, there was an email from her there, jabbing at her. Is this how Alice feels when I message her? Ila thought, before disregarding it. No. That's completely different.

Hey love, wrote Joyce, *I hope you're okay. I'm sorry we got off on the wrong foot the other day. I promise you I'm not usually like that at all, I'd had a bit to drink and the stress of the day had gotten to me.*

Fuck you, she replied. *How did you get my contact details? Fuck you, and never come near me again.*

She covers herself in warm things until she feels cocooned by knitted fabric. Ila leaves her flat to get the bus, which arrives on time out of the greying evening and loops to the outskirts of the city - the other side of the city, nowhere near where the House is waiting, trying to grab at her with its brick-and-mortar nails. The bus shakes with every turn. It's an old bus. There are no USB phone chargers or LED screens telling her what the next stop is, but she knows the route intimately so that doesn't matter. Her parents live at the opposite end of everything, in a fancy little two-bedroom place situated up a hill which is spotted all over with other fancy little two-bedroom places. When people from the city got money, this was where they went. Away from the rabble. Up above the city, so they could look down on it from on high. Up here, as she gets off the bus, the wind is strong. It comes in from the ocean, rolling over the buildings below until it meets her, here, and gets tangled in her hair.

Just outside her parents' front door, she looks down, as long as she can stand. The chill stings her face, but she looks down, seeing the sea as a grey flat desert, and the faded image of an oil tanker passing far out on the other side of a strip of rain. The shore is an irregular line, and then the buildings come thick, the roads a confusing mess of car headlights and streetlights in the rush hour of early evening. She finds it strange that American cities are structured with intention. Grids of right angles, impossible to find yourself lost in, surely. Here the cities are mistakes, towns which grew too big and so conjoined with other towns, swallowing all the villages and the countryside around them whole in their desperate need for more space. She looks down the hill. She follows the line of a main road which winds from the city centre out, pushing its way through estates, parting them like the red sea. Then, it split into two. One of the two new roads rises up and joins the motorway leading away between the hill. She looks to the other fork of the road. Once, a long time ago now, it led to a train station. Now, it does not. The tower block is visible. The lights of people's kitchens and televisions are flickering on as they get home from work. And on the other side of the road, a black splotch. She can't actually see it, not really, just the darkness and the forest around it, but it's there, drawing her eye to it. And across the distance, it calls to her.

Look upon me once again into my eye hello my love.

Shivers run across her skin. The voice is like the voice of an old friend or lover, something speaking from out of her past. She had let it fade from her but now, looking at it across the city, there it came again. Just like it had never left. Just like she had never left its walls.

You miss me don't you?

Does she? No. Of course she doesn't miss it. That's what

she tells herself. How could she miss something so horrible? How could she yearn for that still?

You miss me, don't you?

It asks again. The words are silken.

You miss me.

"Ila?" The trance was broken. Her mum had opened the door and found her there, standing on the pavement outside their house, staring off into the distance. "Ila!" she says, and opens up her arms to embrace her daughter. "Come here!"

She runs to her mother and hugs her deeply, pressing her face into the woman's shoulder. Her shawl is soft on her face, and Ila worries that she might cry.

Their home is warm, filled with the aroma of spices. She lets the rich smell fill her up and calm her head, which still spins from seeing... talking to... being talked to by the House. If that had even been what had happened. The words had not come from within. They had come from the exterior, yet a house cannot speak, it has no voicebox. But it speaks anyway, doesn't it? Your house. It speaks to you. Stop and listen and hear it, the heating, the creaking of the pipes. The house settling is also a way of saying *goodnight.*

Alice used to call Ila's mum a MILF, and she had to admit that she was objectively quite attractive. She was short, like Ila, with long black hair and tits which Ila, thankfully, hadn't inherited. When Ila's mother embraced her, she felt a small, Oedipian impulse to nestle into her mum's breasts and stay there for as long as she could. She felt that then, in the long warming hug, before her mum let go.

Her dad is in the kitchen, sitting at the table on his laptop. "Hello darling," he says, looking up from his screen. "You look a little pale." She rolls her eyes. "I heard you on the radio the other day." He had the clipped BBC English of somebody who had been to Oxford University. Crisp, and perfectly assimilated into white society.

"Oh God... I haven't been able to listen to it. I can't stand hearing my voice."

"No, no, don't be silly!"

He stands up to give her a hug as well. It isn't as long or as warm as the one her mother gave her, but it is a good hug still.

"It was great," he says. "Very... impassioned. I'd love to talk to you about it."

She hopes he will forget to do that. She just wants to be with them, and not have to think about penises for a couple of hours.

While they cook she looks upstairs, saying that she needs to use the loo but actually she just wants to see her childhood bedroom. The parents of missing kids preserve their lost little ones' rooms in the chance that they may, one day, come home. They do this for years, past the point where, if the child had lived, they would have still needed a bedroom at their parents' house, especially not one still covered in all their juvenile interests. Ila's parents have turned her bedroom into an office for her dad. She feels no betrayal at this – they had asked her, after all, if it was okay to do. Yes, she said. I don't mind at all. But it's still surreal to look into the room and see a desk there where her bed used to be. Her father often sits and works now in the same geographic space where she cried herself to sleep as a teenager, or where she cut open her wrists. She once got blood all over her sheets and said that her period had come. They didn't believe her.

The bathroom, too, has changed. It has been repainted in the three years since she attempted suicide, transformed from a baby blue to a burgundy. The bath is a white coffin still speckled with droplets of water from somebody's shower, and she steps into it, fully dressed. Ila lies down in the bath. The slight dampness soaks through her clothes. It is strange to lie in the same point in space where she tried to die. The colour of the walls gets lighter. In the delusion, which she knows is just that: just a delusion, Alice appears, faint in the white hotness of the overhead lightning. Alice there, the red walls behind her, looks towards Ila and becomes Joyce, still gazing upon her body, and Joyce becomes others still. Countless men through her university years that prodded at her, held her against bus stops and kissed her hard until a friend called her name. Men whose hands found their way up her dress in the drunk sweaty closeness of a bar. And beyond that, at school. Older boys making up rumours about her. You know what they say about Jewish girls? They're great at deepthroating. Shall we test that out?

The bath could fill up with every drop of her blood. The blood could splatter over the walls and repaint them red. Like a womb, wet and red, and her, small, pale, lifeless inside of it, curled up at its centre.

Come into me Ila I miss you come sit in my heart for a while beating drink of my lifeblood I miss you you imperfect with your body you hate with my words on you the words I put there and the words I didn't.

Ila's dad knocks on the door.

"Ah, sorry! Won't be long," she says.

"No problem. Just needed to. Um."

She can hear him get embarrassed through the door. When she gets to her feet, they feel weak, but she stands and leans on the wall for a moment to get her balance back. Her arms are fine. The scars on them are faded, the ones which are words almost entirely unreadable. The one on her stomach is legible. She couldn't imagine how it was for her parents when they saw those words there, in scabbed dried blood. Generational trauma carved over her fertility. It must have made them scream with horror. But she had no memory of that. Her body sometimes feels unreal. It surprises her to see it in the mirror.

Ila lets her dad into the toilet and then walks down the stairs, two at a time, suddenly remarkably energetic. She nearly trips over herself as she reaches the bottom, but doesn't fall.

The food is good, a rich chickpea curry with home baked naan, bigger than a plate. Her mum watches her eat with encouraging eyes. Ila knows she's waiting for her to smile and exclaim how delicious it is, which she does, because it is, but also because her mum needs to see that to make her feel like the meal was worth it.

"Have you been busy?" her dad asks, sipping his post-dinner coffee.

Ila stifles a shrug. She worries he would think it was rude in some way, so she just makes a noncommittal noise and says, "Oh, not really. I've been writing a bit I guess."

"Seeing anyone?" her mum asks.

Sigh. Does being nearly-raped by a woman in some pub toilets count as *seeing someone*? Probably not.

"I'm not really in a place for that right now."

Because every time she fucks anyone it feels wrong, and she sees herself from the outside like a voyeur looking through a hole drilled in the wall.

Because most people she matches with on Her turn out to be fucking TRAs.

"I read that piece you wrote," her dad says, as if he could tell exactly why she isn't in the place to be dating right now.

"Which piece?"

"The, um..." she can see that he's searching for a way to phrase it. "The piece on the, genre of pornography."

"Sissification?" she says. There's an embarrassment and a thrill in saying something like that in front of her parents.

"Yes that's the one," he says, "you know I have a colleague who is actually a scholar of pornography throughout history. Very underrepresented field, very interesting, actually."

Her mum says nothing. She doesn't even look at either of them, just stares down at her empty plate, and her coffee.

"I, I'm not sure about that. Because I don't agree with the whole thing. Pornography. I think it exploits women."

Her dad nodded. "Yes, I read that bit, at the end. From Dworkin. But I just don't really understand what the point of these videos is."

The thrill of talking about such an illicit subject in front of her parents has now faded to complete embarrassment. Now she just hopes that he leaves it alone. But she knows her father too well to really believe that he will.

"What's the point of them, Ila?"

"I'm... are you sure I should say that at the dinner table?"

"We're not puritanical, babe, don't be silly. We don't mind at all, do we?"

Ila's mum doesn't say anything for a moment, and then realises she missed her cue. She looks up and smiles, saying of course they don't mind, no, of course they aren't puritanical at all.

"Well basically," Ila is treading carefully through the conversation, finding that it is practically forged from barbed wire. "The whole deal with it is that these men look at these videos, and, well, the videos are all about trying to hypnotise them into thinking, or realising, that they're women. Does that make sense?"

"But they're not women?" Her dad asks.

"No. No, they're not."

"Okay, let me be a... a sort of devil's advocate here. There's a trans woman who teaches at my work. She's a brilliant scholar, and she was given a prize for being the best female scholar of the year. But you would think that she shouldn't have gotten that?"

"No, not at all. Give her a prize for being a trans scholar or something. But giving her that prize now means that one woman is locked out, of the money and the prestige that she could have gotten from that."

"But she *is* a woman," says her dad. "That's the thing I don't get, I mean. She is a woman."

"I don't think we should talk about this anymore." Ila says it abruptly, and a silence descends on the dining room table. The evening ends on a sour note. Ila doesn't stay for much longer; she has to write a lot tomorrow; she has to pitch articles and things like that. She should get some rest.

Her mother gives her one last deep hug at the door, before she steps out into the cold. Things have gotten dark now. The city glimmers with a hundred thousand yellow points of light. She can feel the pull from the left to turn her head and look down at the spot where no light shines, but she keeps her eyes firmly away, anywhere but there.

Your father is wrong.

She starts to walk down the road towards the bus stop, looking at her feet as they hit the pavement.

Your father is wrong of course you know he is wrong I know you know that I understand.

The bus stop has a little digital sign, saying that her bus will be there in ten minutes. She stands beneath it. Cars spin past, some blaring rap out of their windows, one or two blaring out classical music. Fuck, she should have brought headphones. Why didn't she bring headphones?

Tell me about why your father is wrong, Ila.

The House isn't even visible from here. She has crested the hill and gone over. It isn't a voice in her head. She has heard voices in her head, long ago when she was about fifteen. This isn't that; this voice belongs only to the House. At first, outside her parents' house, she thought it sounded like a lover, but now it makes her think of a lecturer she used to have at university, who spoke so beautifully that she could barely understand anything the woman was saying, she was so enrapt in the way it was said.

Listen to me now. Listen and do what I say. Come home Ila, whispers the House, *your parents are not your home not at all you felt more at home inside me than you ever had within their walls I know what you want you want to take it out on her don't you you know what she did and you hate her and you want to punish.*

Ila screws her eyes shut tightly. The House circles her like a panther. It wants to kiss her, deep and wet, push its tongue between her lips.

The bus comes, and she thrusts her way onto it, nearly falling over in her rush. The driver is confused. She's the only person getting on, and almost all of the seats are free. The words on her stomach pulsate. Alice once made them watch a film, all three of them, Alice, her, and Hannah, when they were drunk. She wouldn't say what it was, and then the title card came up. It was *Ilsa, She Wolf of the SS.* Alice had kissed her and called her Ila, She Wolf of the SS later on and Ila had screamed at her. Their first real fight. Their first real hate-fuck. The first line of many crossed. The words on her and in her make themselves known, and she itches at them, but inside the bus, the voice of the House seems to fade away, or give up. The longer she sits there leaning against the window, the vibration of the vehicle's movement replaces the strange feeling that had come from within.

That night she smokes weed on her balcony, listening to seagulls whirling through the air above. They didn't seem to take any kind of notice what time of day it was. Their screams were constant. You are by the sea, they said, even if you cannot see the sea from here.

Here is your custom video, says the email notification. It's not to her main email account, but a side one, which doesn't use her real name. She opens it, puts in her earphones, and clicks on the streaming link.

The video shows a transwoman. It isn't Alice, but, for a moment, you could think that it was. They're both white with curly brown hair and thick eyebrows. But this transwoman has blue eyes and higher cheekbones. It's not Alice. That would be too far, she thinks, covertly paying Alice for something like this.

"Now listen to me," says the transwoman in the video, fifty pounds up from the transaction. She thinks that Ila is a man called Harry, who dreams of being a sissy. Ila's head is floating with the weed. Every word feels like a kiss. She isn't sure if, to her disgust, she's horny, or feels sick. Her hand goes between her legs anyway. "Now listen to me Harry," says the transwoman on the little screen, "I know all about you. It's okay. Breathe slowly. Do everything I say from now on, is that clear? Say yes, so I know."

Without thinking, Ila says it aloud: "Yes."

HOUSE

They built the House well, with the finest of materials, with the finest stone and timber that could be sourced. A good house, raised up against the elements, with the dark of the forest at its back and the new world approaching from the front. A house of progress, went the thought process. But something had gone wrong, there. It became sick. You made it sick, didn't you? You, with your ideas, with your thoughts. You saw the House and called it fascist, and you did this enough that, eventually, it became one.

No. Of course that wasn't how it happened. That isn't how a fascist is made, only how people think a fascist is made.

The man who commissioned the House was named William Martin. He was a proud man with good blood pumping through his veins. His father was a politician, and so he became a politician too. He spared no expense when it came to the architects and the builders. William pored over the blueprints every time he got the chance, his eyes alight with dreams of this new house. This new house needed a name, but he couldn't think of one. How to choose a name for a house? Choosing a name for a child was hard enough, but a house... a house would live longer than any person, and a name would construct its whole personality.

"Well, do you have any ideas?" he asked the young man. They were in a room in the upstairs of a building in Soho, with heavy black curtains on its windows. The room smelled of perfume which emanated from the bath water, from the candles, and from the young man himself. William liked to press his face close into him and take a deep breath of that sweet scent that came from his skin, and the young man would laugh.

"Well," said the sweet-smelling boy. He was very young. Barely sixteen, no facial hair, no hair on his body apart from the black mass curling around his genitals. William would pick those hairs from his teeth with a smile. Their limbs were pressed together in the copper bath, the water still steaming. "You said that there is a forest near to the house?"

"Why, yes. Stretching up the hill, as far as the eye can see."

"What are the types of trees that are in the forest?"

William thought. "I am not sure. Beech trees, I think. No, Beech House, that doesn't sound right at all."

"Then the village near. What do they call that?"

"I am not sure it is even a village, my boy. It's so small. Just a collection of houses and fishing huts and one little inn, is all."

"But what do they call it?"

"Well, you know, I think you have something there."

He leaned over and kissed the young man long and deep on the mouth, and he moved one of the young man's hands until it was touching his hard prick under the hot water.

So they called the House the name it still calls itself, but which time itself has forgotten. Even if everyone else only calls it the House, the House knows, and addresses itself as it would like to be addressed.

I am Albion, says the House, proudly. *And Albion is within me.*

But before Albion could exist, it stalled. It was built, mostly, by this time. But as they were filling out the insides with all sorts of wonderful trinkets, a letter came to the builders to say that there would be no need to continue. William Martin had been arrested for buggery, and was in prison, starving. He was refusing to eat anything at all. He had been part of a ring of men who would pass boys between them. One of those boys had been paid by a rival politician to tell the police about this, and they had caught him, quite literally red handed. William Martin was the only man prosecuted for the affair. He starved to death before he could be sentenced to anything. His wife was distraught. Her own husband. She got a carriage to the shell of Albion, abandoned now, the place which was to be her wedded paradise. Now her husband was skin and bones, and all of society knew her as the wife of a deviant. The House, Albion, looked down at her as she left the carriage and walked between its gates. The place was silent. The workmen had gone and taken anything of use that they could retrieve. She pushed open its door, which hadn't even been locked. Inside, it was half built. The stairs were rudimentary, and the roof was open to the elements. Birds nested at the top of the walls. There were no portraits or treasures, of course. They would have been moved in just before her and William. The House was an abortion, and she hated it with every fibre of herself. The House hated her back. It hated her and her deviant husband. It had sat there during his hearings, stewing with resentment at its un-being. It blamed the woman, too.

How could you not know?

"Of course I didn't know," said the woman, looking at the House's empty insides.

My body is half formed a halfformedthing, said the House, *but climb up my insides onto my first floor.*

"Why?"

I have something that I would like to show you.

She did so. The stairs that existed there were dangerous, and she thought she was going to fall. But the House wanted her to go up them, and so up them she went. Onto the first floor.

"And now where?"

There is only one corridor which they have finished building. Many of the rooms down it are open to the air. One is not. It will be easy to find.

It was obvious which corridor the House meant. It was to her right. Outside, it started to rain, and rain dripped through the roof, making the wood swell sickly. Mrs Martin walked down the dark corridor. There were doorways on each side, but the rooms were empty, many without windows or with holes in the roof. None of them were the room at the heart of Albion.

She knew it when she saw it. A door at the end of the corridor, the only door down the length of the whole thing. She walked up to it, and then found herself hesitating.

Push open the door, and you will find the answers to your husband's condition. You will know everything you need to. You will, if you try hard enough, be able to bring him back, cured of his... ills.

"What you are saying," she said, "is impossible."

I am so much more than you will ever be. I can do so much more. I am the terror at the heart of this country, and I can tell this country what to do. I have been built new from the blood and guts of endless sin and now I sit upon this pile of misshapen skulls and I laugh at my newfound land.

It took a long time for anyone to find her. She was hanging in one of the empty rooms that came off of that corridor, one of the ones with a roof open to the sky. By that time her body had rotted. Her stomach was open to the elements, and things were within it, nesting. Bits of her had dropped to the ground and been chewed at by animals. They took her away and buried her. The House remained. More would come to it, and soon. It was good real estate. People would buy it, or the land it was built upon. It would live.

I am Albion.

Albion is all that is within me.

And within me is all of Albion.

ALICE

The beach is cold, so I shuffle even closer to the fire, close enough that it threatens to singe my clothes but I stay there anyway, letting it warm me. In my pocket my phone is buzzing – Jon's asking me *come on Alice when are you coming over* but I don't open the message. I have to do this first. The sky is dark already. Nobody comes down to the beach out of season at night. In the heat of summer, after the Pride Parade has dispersed, people come down here and swim, and sit on the hot pebbles long into the night, sometimes staying until the sun comes up back up again. I did that with Ila and Hannah, once. We built a fire and stocked up on bottles of Buckfast. The Pride Parade was exhausting every year but that year, the last one we had together, it had been boiling hot. We marched, although we weren't really allowed. Not just the three of us, a whole group, protesting something or other, some bank's involvement in the parade. There were enough of us that when security came and tried to pull one of us out, the rest of us closed around like a shield. We were hot, passionate, and kept each other as safe as we could. Burning under the sun, shouting *the first Pride was a riot, first Pride was a riot, where's a brick when you need it? first pride was a riot.*

But afterwards we slipped down here. We ordered pizza to the beach and, to our delight, it was actually delivered. We built a fire, bigger than the one I made tonight, and watched as groups all along to the left and to the right built them too. It got dark. The fire burned bright, making Ila look so astoundingly beautiful. The flames flickered, reflecting in her eyes. I sat opposite her, the fire in between us, Hannah off to the side, toasting marshmallows. Ila was looking at her, talking about something I don't remember. Her look for Pride was glitter covering her face and her cleavage. It sparkled, now, sparkled a deep orange. She smiled, and then looked at me. She knew I'd been looking.

But later, Hannah fell asleep next to the fire, which had dimmed down to just embers. We lay there with her, not wanting to wake her but not wanting to leave her either. We pressed together to stay warm. We were always drunk when we fucked, and that time was no different, of course. Out in the open air, the rawness of it was astounding. Hannah snoring next to us. Hundreds of people on the beach doing the same, engaging in their most basic queer lust. Ila's mouth tickled my neck and down my chest as she pulled the buttons on my dress open and wormed her hands inside. Her fingers cold. My thighs warm. The Buckfast in our heads making the world spin. Hannah didn't wake up, she never knew. I wonder if it was bad. She didn't consent to being there with us.

I grip a picture of the three of us together from that day. In the photo we are close and smiling, our skin going red after all that sun. On the beach the moon is full above my head, ready to burst in a bright shower of scolding hot liquid silver. It is the time for the destruction of old things, and the manifestation of the new. I hold the picture close enough to the flames for it to catch. Immediately, all of my senses are telling me to drop it, but I don't. I raise it up, letting the fire shoot up from the photograph as long as I dare until the heat begins to burn. Then I let go. The picture loops up through the air, crests, then begins to fall. When it tumbles down, it does so further out, over the sea now. Its light flickers until it reaches the water, where it vanishes.

I have more pictures. Every picture of the three of us, in fact. All the ones which hid beneath my bed. Now the poster is gone, I can push things away, cleanse myself and my space. The pictures are a bundle, with a rubber band holding them together. That first one I afforded a dramatic send off, but these I just drop into the fire. It eats them there in front of my eyes.

It's a pleasure to burn.

There's only one last thing here, at the bottom of my bag: a book of Adrienne Rich's *Selected Poems*. On the title page, Ila wrote: *to Alice, my instrument in the shape of a woman.* It was a birthday gift. A week before this we had fucked for the first time, and neither of us knew what we wanted from it. Were we friends who fucked, or girlfriends? When she gave the book to me, I thanked her and kissed her cheek, but later, out in the smoking area of the pub we were in, I asked her what she'd meant by giving me that book, of all the possible books she could have gifted.

"What do you mean? I didn't mean anything." She was tipsy, defensive.

"Come on," I said, "you really don't know?"

"No!" Ila seemed offended.

I sighed. "She was sort of a TERF. Like, an early one. She was friends with Janice Raymond, who wrote *The Transsexual Empire*."

TERF wasn't quite as widely used when we had this conversation, it has ballooned in the past few years, as a term, as a front of the culture war, but Ila knew what it meant. Back then, of course, she would never have dreamed of thinking of herself as one. In *The Transsexual Empire,* Raymond quotes Rich decrying transsexuals as "men who have given up the supposed ultimate possession of manhood in a patriarchal society by self-castration." And she thinks this is, I suppose, a bad thing. Which is strange, because in that quote it can almost seem like a positive. That trans women are radical for literally cutting the manhood away from them to be free of violent patriarchy. But no. I guess not. I guess it couldn't be, not to her.

"Fuck, really?" Ila looked upset. "God, no, I didn't realise. Sorry. Sorry, I promise it was an accident."

I shrugged. "I like her poetry, though. It was a lovely gift. Really."

Now, I throw the book, with Rich's face in black and white on the cover, into the flames. She burns too, and the words inside it, and the note Ila wrote in biro.

The sea is approaching, and, before long, it will wash over the fire and take away the ash that remains of the memories. I stand up and walk back up the beach with my back to it all.

Jon and Sasha are having people over. He's been texting me, asking me when I'm going to come, for the past two hours, and finally I respond that I'm free now and on my way. Their place isn't far from the beach, but, to be fair, most places in the city aren't far from each other. It is small and dense. But there are outskirts, little places that were once separate villages but have been swallowed up. They are further, scattered around between small pockets of countryside. Between small pockets of trees, and then there, at the very edge, the forest.

It doesn't take me long to get to Jon and Sasha's. I haven't seen them since the party where I picked up Sabi, and have, to be honest, been neglecting our friendship. When I respond to their messages I offer short, closed-off responses that don't leave space for further talk. I've been isolated since the Sabi thing. And alone, in my room, now the poster is gone and the only face I have to look at is Hannah's face in the stains, which I keep telling myself I should call my landlord about, say hey, there's damp on the wall shaped like the face of a girl I knew who died, can you come and get rid of it?

People don't seem to remember Hannah anymore. I do, of course. But the world at large... no one ever asks about her. There was, of course, a search. But it faded.

As soon as the house ate her, it began to eat the memory of her, too. I wonder if her family think about her much at all. They did broadcasts telling her to come home, but she had already gone home. Dead or missing girls, especially early twenties white girls, are dime a dozen and always popular fodder for mystery podcasts or Netflix documentaries. But in Hannah's case there's been nothing.

Jon and Sasha live in an apartment above a pub that's always closed. It's hard to find the door, and the buzzer, which you have to press, but I've been there enough that I know it. It's around this little corner, here. It seems a bit scary, if you don't know it, like you're being lured somewhere under false pretences, because the corner that the door is in is permanently shadowed even during the day. Nobody has ever bothered to put in a streetlight here. I go up the couple of steps and press the buzzer, which is low, worrying about whether they heard it over their music. The thought comes again, quicker this time. Maybe I should just turn around and head home. Maybe that would be better. But the door opens. It's Leon, glimmering with new blonde hair and golden eyeshadow.

"Hey, Alice!" he says, and grabs me in a burst of unexpected affection. I feel him kiss my cheeks and leave a slight pink lipstick mark on them, then he ushers me inside, to hang my coat on a hook. There are a lot of coats there. It's hard to balance mine on top of the others on the same hook, but I manage it just about, I think. I don't know where these coats come from. Do Jon and Sasha own that many? Or, the far worse possibility, are there more people here than I thought?

"So Alice, how have you been?" asks Leon over his shoulder as we head up the stairs to the main part of the flat. *Well, Leon,* I say in my head, *my hook-up ran out on me after being attacked by a ghost possessing a picture of a cancelled 80s pop singer, I made some sissification porn, and my rapist tried to get in contact again.* I don't say that. I say: "Oh, you know. I've been sleeping a lot. Just felt so tired most days I can barely get out of bed." Which isn't a lie. "What about you?"

"Well," Leon jumps up the last few steps. "I've been trying to get back to doing linoprint, which is fun but god you cut up your fingers so much, see—" he shows me his hands for a moment, which have shallow scabbed-over cuts all over them "—but I find it really rewarding to return to something like that, that I used to do at school, but with my new perspectives, you know."

"Aliiiiiiice," calls Jon. He's leaning in the doorway. I'm surprised to see that he, too, is wearing eyeliner, and lipstick as well. "How are you ma love?" He kisses my cheek. I must look like an old cartoon of a man covered in kisses. Sasha pushes past Jon and kisses me too.

We've never been affectionate like this before. I look around and realise what I should have known from the number of coats. It isn't just the three of them here. Other people, in groups, are clustered about the living room and the kitchen. Even as I'm trying to find somewhere to stash my bag the buzzer goes again. Some of the people, with faces I half recognise, look over at me in the middle of their disparate conversations. Can they tell there's something wrong with me – is there something wrong with the way I look, or is it just because I'm trans and the only trans girl here and fuck, I didn't realise this was going to be a real, full on party. If I had, I'm not sure I'd have come. Maybe that's why they didn't tell me. The thought of being in a throng of sweaty, drugged up bodies again is making me shake. I need to be out of my head, or this is going to go badly. It might go badly anyway, even with me out of my head. I brought some wine, and swig it from the bottle, trying to get to a level of drunk that makes the situation more palatable. The wine bottle is half empty before I start to calm down.

Their flat is too big, far too big for a flat in this part of the city. God, I know Jon's parents are rich, but this is obscene. The living room is like a cavern, and there's a dining room connected onto the kitchen, and a balcony outside, where people have already started to gather. Does he know all of these people? Are they friends, or have they just smelled the scent of booze and coke and come clawing at the door until somebody lets them in? Sasha is sitting on the couch, and I sit down next to her.

"You okay?" she says. She's holding a glass of something very strong and lets me take a sip through the same straw that she's been using. Strong and sweet. She puts her arm over my shoulder. "Alice, are you okay?"

"I just didn't realise there would be a lot of people here." Even as I say that I can see, through the archway of the living room door, three girls have arrived in short tight dresses.

"Didn't Jon tell you?" Sasha asks.

"No, he just said he was having a couple of people over. Not a whole party." I try to laugh but it sounds about as forced as it is.

"Tell you what," says Sasha, "we set up a chillout room upstairs. I'll take you up there and you can come down when you're feeling a bit better. How's that?"

"Yeah, sure, yeah. That sounds great."

There's a second layer to the flat, a further floor with smaller rooms up a smaller staircase near the kitchen. The stairway that leads up there, which she guides me up, is almost too tight for me to cope with. But the room itself is larger. Not too large, not a looming empty space, but not claustrophobic. Sasha sets me up on a beanbag in the room. It smells like incense, and there's a mood light transitioning from green to blue.

"I have to go back down," says Sasha, "call me if you need to though, and hope you can join us soon."

It feels horrifically embarrassing, being left here on the soft bean bag with a half empty bottle of wine. Kids parties have chillout rooms. There's music playing from a laptop up on a desk in the corner. I can't tell what this room is when it isn't a *chillout room*. An office? The roof is slanted and practically cuts off half of the headspace. The quiet, electronic music feels like it is stuck on a loop. I swear, the moment one piece ends, it starts again. An endless electronic squeal.

The mood lighting goes to yellow, then orange, and then, slowly, darkens until everything is bathed in red. The computer and the crooked ceiling. Me, too. I can see myself in a mirror up above the table. My face, washed out by the red light so that my features are barely visible. Just a faceless red girl. In a red room.

This is worse than being in the party. But when I try to lift myself off of the beanbag my legs don't work. Fuck, I think, fuck I haven't drunk that much, I haven't taken anything, I... I look up, and I see Ila on the other side of the room. The mood lightning should have changed by now, transitioned to purple, then blue, then green again, but it stays red, it stays red and quivers around us. You and I, Ila. The music sounds like screaming infused through a synthesiser. This is not a ghost. Ila is not dead, and this house is not haunted. Well, of course it is. Every house is haunted. But it doesn't haunt me. Yet Ila stands there, on the other side of the room. She doesn't move. I can't move either.

And then, as fast as she arrived, she's gone. I raise myself to my feet, feeling unsteady, and grab the wine to drink more of it. The mood light seems to be stuck on red. I don't want to be in that place a second longer, so I leave as fast as I can without tripping on the steep stairwell. The synth music fades away behind me, and below me a thumping bass reaches up, mixed with voices – so many voices. Too many. I descend into them and come out near the kitchen. There are so many people here now. More people than my brain can readily take in. More voices saying more words than I can grasp on to. People dancing and snogging and laughing. In the middle of them I spot Leon, his eyes pointed at the ceiling, and fight my way through towards him. People are unwilling to move for me. As I try to weave around them, eyes glare at me. Who the fuck do I think I am?

I have no idea how long I was in the chillout room. I thought I was only ten minutes but in my absence the party's entire being has changed. I call out to Leon when I get close, and he sees me. My arms are pointing out. He grabs one and jerks me to him.

"Hey!" His eyes are white disks.

"What's happening? Where did all these people come from?"

"I don't know!" He smiles. "Someone who knows someone told a Whatsapp group, and they told more people, and now look at it, look at all these people! Do you have any coke?"

"No," I say, "sorry!" He must have already run out. Where's Sasha?"

"In her bedroom!"

I know where that is. It's on the other side of the crowd, though. The crowd of strangers. How can I have lived in this city for so long, and have been to so many parties, and recognise so few of these people? The ones I do feel like I've seen before aren't people I would talk to. I don't even know a lot of their names. I have to use my shoulder to try and pry my way through people. Someone tells me to fuck off when I knock them off balance, I say sorry, sorry, and pull them up, but they shove me away, into five other people, who spill their drinks on each other, and then they push me away too, into more people. Hands on me, jostling me until they knock me nearly off my feet. I'm scrambling across the floor, and the door is in sight. The bedroom. I can be safe in the bedroom. Sasha will know what to do, and Jon, if he's there as well. I'm sure he didn't mean to invite this many people.

The door opens beneath my hands. Inside, the bedroom is dark. The atmosphere is moist with sweat, so moist my skin feels condensation settling upon it. I don't see them at first. But then I do, although it's hard for me to really recognise what it actually is that I've stumbled into. On the bed, Jon is sitting on an unconscious Sasha. Her head tips forwards, bending down over the edge of the bed.

"Fucking amazing party out there," Jon says. He straddles her back. Her dress is pulled down, and he has a knife in his right hand. On the skin of her left shoulder, he has inscribed words with the blade, which seep blood out onto the bedcovers. The knife has blood along its pale edge.

Ila, over me, cutting into my forehead. Jon never commented on it, but he must have seen the pale pussy scar. I try to hide it, but it's impossible to do completely.

Jon, with his knife fetish. Sasha, eyes closed, mouth open but wordless. I can see now, even in the dim light. Her exposed back is riddled with them; with Jon's words, so many of them that in some parts of her the scars are layered one over the other. Over and over. And there, the freshest one, newly cut just a minute ago. They all say the same thing: *Property of Jon Harroway.*

Jon stands up, and steps off his girlfriend. He jumps athletically off the bed and walks slowly towards me. The knife swings loosely at his side, but it is, very much, *there*. He knows I'm eyeing it.

"Alice," he says, "don't tell anyone, okay?"

"No." I gulp, or try to. My throat is dry. I left my wine somewhere. If I was holding it, I'd feel safer, knowing I had something I could use for defence. But there's nothing in my hands. "No, of course not."

"It's completely consensual."

I look at her.

"She asks me for it. I keep telling her it isn't safe, but it's the only way she can get off, you know?"

"I understand."

"So if you walk out of here now, you're not going to try and misrepresent this, are you?"

"No, Jon. Why would I do that? What you and Sasha do together is your own business."

He nods. "Amazing."

I can't get out of the bedroom fast enough, or back through the violent, angry crowds fast enough. I don't see Leon but I know he is somewhere amidst them, grinning to himself. I hope he found some coke. I retrieve my bag from under the chair where I left it, elbowing people to get to it, and then scramble for the stairs down to the door. When I get to the coat rack, mine has fallen off of the hook into a crumpled heap on the floor. People entering the party have stepped on it carelessly. So many people. Packed like animals in a battery farm. I put the coat on anyway. When I'm outside, in the cold air again, I start to dry heave into the gutter, and at the same time I cry. Both forces push their way up through my body and make it spasm, almost uncontrollably. I lean against the wall of the dead pub. What if he kills her? What if he kills her and I didn't tell anyone? What if I tell someone and he kills me?

My phone buzzes.

Ila is there again.

I need to talk to you, she says. *Can we please meet? In a public place? I really, really need to talk with you.*

ILA

Ila usually likes to smoke on her balcony but it's too cold today, so she's put a sock over the fire alarm and is smoking while lying in bed, ashing into a cereal bowl, feeling like a boy. She scrolls through Twitter on her laptop, just for the action of scrolling, barely reading anything at all. Every tweet on her timeline is decrying Brexit, or this court case relating to Stonewall, or the horror of autogynephilia. After a while they all seem to blur into one. An echo chamber of the same outrage repeating for eternity in the white expanse of Online.

After doing this for long enough that the boredom starts to gnaw at her, she switches to another website, a forum which was originally meant to be used for women to discuss motherhood but which has now become the de facto internet meeting place of gender criticals. It feels weird, though, typing in the website's name. She is nobody's mother, and she never will be. There's a thread called *TRANS WIDOWS ESCAPE COMMITTEE PART 5* which she clicks on. There's always something darkly hilarious about these ones. They're for people who are married, or were married, to someone who came out as trans to air their grievances. So she reads, each little confession a snapshot of someone with a sadder life than her.

USER 1 (Unidentified): *My husband began to insist on being referred to as a woman. He took over childcare roles and he cooked for me most nights. He would dress up in a dress and heels and makeup and clean the house and I could see he was getting off on that. I could see his dick was hard poking through the dress.*

USER 2 (Unidentified): *Mine dresses up but doesn't seem interested in the labour aspect of womanhood, would prefer it if he did do all that really.*

USER 1: *No this is worse.*

USER 3 (Unidentified): *He forgot our anniversary. Says it was the hormones clouding his brain. Bulls###. He never remembered anything beforehand. I was always having to remind him of his own mother's birthday. Oftentimes I brought her a present too and said it was from the two of us. And now he forgot our anniversary. He shaves and leaves the mess of the stubble in the sink.*

(When Alice was still a teenager, and had just come out, she did this. She still lived at home, and her mum found the sink still covered in little bits of facial hair which she had shaved off. Her mum made her clean the sink and called her a boy.)

(When Ila was about sixteen, a girl in her maths class made fun of her for her darker facial hair. Ila cried when she got home, the girl had called her a man... she looked in the mirror and saw a man, in a kind fantasy, looking back at her.

She took a shower and dreamed that she was a man, a penis pushing through her pussy lips, thick hairs pushing through her chest. She got out of the shower and tried to shave her face, but, because the mirror was misted-up, she cut her top lip with the razor. The blood dripped down and filled her mouth up with that metallic taste.)

Ila often wonders where Alice is now, what she is doing. Whenever she texts or emails late at night, she is particularly high or in a semi-dream state. Alice has a few social media accounts that Ila checks up on semi-regularly, but most of them are rarely updated. There's a Twitter account under Alice's name, and she looks at the *likes* tab but there are only very occasionally any new things there that she's paid attention to. It seems likely that Alice has other accounts on other websites that she doesn't know about. The Alice that Ila can see on the internet is a loose, faded impression. *Like a ghost.* Well, not really anything like a ghost at all. Ghosts are consistent. They appear at regular intervals, but Alice seems to appear at random. Ila only has one Twitter account. It is followed by three *Guardian* journalists, a well-known television writer, and a famous children's author. She logs onto it and tweets a picture at a charity. The picture is of a transwoman holding a baseball bat coloured with the Trans Pride Flag. She tweets the picture at the charity, asking *is this what you defend? Are these people really harmless to women?* and gets retweets from people with names like JennyXX, but also replies from people telling her to shut up, *shut the fuck up TERF go deal with your own dysphoria.*

The last time Ila fucked a girl, she wore a strap-on – a big, realistic, black silicone cock with balls and veins – and black piece of ribbon tied around her abdomen to cover her scars. She fucked the girl from behind, and then flipped her over, bent her legs up to her shoulder, and went deeper with the cock. She felt at one with the strap-on, then. As the girl yelled "I love your cock!" it became the most natural thing in the world that yes, she had a cock, of course she did. It was part of her, and always had been, as natural as all of her fingers. The girl's moans were the type to push themselves up through her entirely involuntary. She had no control. Ila had control.

She found herself, without thinking, putting her hand around this girl's throat, tracing images on her face with her mind. She could feel her nerve endings growing with each thrust, extending like the roots of a tree out into the cock. It was painful at first but then, with a jolt, there was the pleasure, sharp and clear in her lower half. She had a cock, and the cock had always been there. She could even feel the girl, tight and wet, all around her cock, despite its artificiality. Ila looked down at the girl, and her face changed, into a different face, her eyes into different eyes, the room they were in morphed, the walls fell away to reveal the bloody flesh underneath, and—

Without warning, the girl pushed her off violently, screaming, and she jumped back.

"What the *fuck* is wrong with you?" said the girl after she'd stopped screaming. Her blonde hair was plastered to her face. She was on her knees on the bed but backing away fast.

"What are you talking about?" asked Ila.

The girl had gotten to the edge of the bed. She jumped off and ran to the other side of the room, panting. Ila was still kneeling there on her sheets, her cock wiggling slightly, back and forth in the air. That connection she had felt to it was gone, like it had simply never been there at all.

The girl looked like she was going to be sick. She touched her neck, like Ila had choked her properly. There are ways of choking during sex, and there are ways of choking that mean you want someone hurt. The girl's neck was bright red.

"You fucking," she spoke with difficulty, between breaths, "you called me a... why the fuck would you even do that? You're sick."

"I don't know what I said!" Ila truly didn't. She didn't remember saying anything at all.

"You called me a tranny. What the fuck. I'm not even trans. What the fuck, Ila."

Ila's trauma has repeated many times over. Or, more accurately, Ila has repeated her trauma. There had been traumas within her before the House had come along and consumed them, but ever since, what happened in the red beating heart of the House had been the focus of all of her fixations. In the fantasies, which were almost identical to the memories that she had, she had always been underneath, with Alice pulling her legs apart, looming over her with the light behind her head. Like a halo. Her face all bathed in red, red in her eyes, red dripping from her mouth. That is what the memories always were. Sometimes, while masturbating, her thoughts turned to them too, and they became fantasies without her wanting them to. In those, as well, it was always the same. Alice on top, pushing into her, her whole body prone and ready to be manipulated. But now she realised, with horror, that she had switched it. She had been on top. In the confusing haze of please, Alice had been there, beneath her, instead of the woman who was now standing terrified against her bedroom wall. She'd been thinking about pushing into Alice's helpless being. She'd called her a tranny.

This had never happened. She hadn't raped Alice, she was certain of that. She was as sure as anything that she had been the victim and was the survivor, but now, fuck, the girl was getting dressed, grabbing her clothes from the places they had been thrown in the wild fucking passion that seemed so impossible now. She stormed from Ila's place, not looking back. Ila ran after her, completely forgetting that she was still completely naked apart from the ribbon around her waist and the strap-on. She ran down the hallway frantically, and was halfway to the front door, which had just slammed behind the girl, when she realised. Ila turned back to her bedroom, sadly. She pulled the ribbon away and looked at her naked body in the mirror, the big black cock still covering her cunt. They had sold out of realistic brown cocks at the shop and she had thought well this isn't so bad, is it, and paid sheepishly. But it looked all wrong there, in the mirror. ARBEIT MACHT FREI carved into her stomach and then, just underneath it, a big cock, still slick with the wetness of another person. All over Ila's limbs were pale scars, some of which looked like undiscernible words or images, some of which were just business-like cuts. Her legs were unshaven. Her armpits were growing good and dark like roses. Her pubic hair was ripe too, it looked like the cock was growing hair around its base.

The cock started to go flaccid before her eyes. No it didn't, of course it didn't. It was made of silicone, and silicone did not go flaccid. It is not part of her. It's a tool. She unstrapped it and let it fall onto the carpet with a dull thud. It was still wet and sticky, and gathered fibres there.

Now here she is, posting on Mumsnet, pretending to be the mother of a little girl who wants to be a boy. *When I was little* she writes *I used to be a tomboy too I would always much rather be down the bottom of the garden playing with worms than watching princess films but now her school must have told her about trans and she wants to mutilate herself she doesn't even have breasts but she already wants them gone... there's a teacher who is a trans identified male at her school could this be down to him?*

Ila never posts as herself on this website, because she's not a mother. But she likes the attention and affirmation she gets from everyone on there, even if the stories she tells are completely fictional.

Same says a reply to her fiction *and I would be wary of the TIM teacher. TIM's are predisposed to being paedophiles you know.*

You can't say that! says another user. *Come on we're all here to be rational you can't go around just making things up like that.*

Sorry replies the one who accused transwomen of being

paedophiles *I'm just saying the truth we all know it though don't we come on it's the truth.*

If you keep talking like that you'll get us banned you daft bint.

Next to her on the bed, Ila's phone suddenly bursts into panicked life. She looks at it, like it is a strange creature that she is unsure is safe to approach. But then she sees the words on the screen, and knows that no. It is unsafe to approach. She picks the phone up slowly and looks at the screaming notifications that come tumbling in over Twitter and through her email, and texts, too, one or two at first, and then a whole flood.

Is it true? Is it true Ila? Did this really happen? Jesus Christ you make me sick I thought better from you.

She scrolls down. She can't actually work out what has happened. Nobody is saying. They're just talking around the subject. But fuck, the thought's there, isn't it. What if? What if: Alice has come forward, told people about what she did, no, what Alice says she did, it didn't really happen surely, she knows that, she *knows.* She didn't rape Alice. This is like a mantra. A grounding wire. If Alice has said that, then she can deny it, and she can be truthful in that denial because she will know she is genuinely, from the heart, saying the honest-to-God truth.

But it isn't Alice. In some ways that would have been easier to cope with. The Alice that lived in her head was barely a person now and had become something closer to a monster from a horror picture, some psycho man who wears women's skin, or dresses as his mother. But it isn't Alice, it's Joyce, the bespectacled gender critical lady from the pub toilets. She tweeted the accusation out into the abyss @*ilafurvors* (which is her username) *after the meeting @ilafurvors approached me in the toilet and tried to initiate sex. I told her I was flattered but she was much too young for me but she kept pushing.* Then a second tweet *I kept asking her to please stop but she pushed me into a stall and assaulted me. I can't believe someone who is part of our movement would do this.*

The fucking bitch. How dare she. After what she'd done, after Ila promised to not tell anyone, she does this, for no reason, no reason at all. Apart from to insure against the possibility that Ila might break that promise. Ila is still high, far too high for this. The phone screen is sharp against her eyes. More words pouring in, asking her if it's true, which is pointless because it isn't. But Joyce has so much more power than her, and she got there first; if you hear an accusation against someone then that biases you, even if the accused leverages a counter accusation.

Is it true? She tweets anyway, despite how pointless it is. *No, it isn't true. In fact, Joyce has accused me of something that SHE DID TO ME. or tried to, at least. She pushed me into a bathroom stall after that exact meeting.*

She can barely read the words, and her breaths are short and not bringing enough oxygen to her brain to think properly. And then she is tagged in something, from a different corner. In the replies to a tweet that says *that accusation is probably true because Ila Sunder attacked me and tried to penetrate me anally nonconsensually six months ago during sex and then when I resisted she called me a transphobic slur.* It's the girl, the one who freaked out on her. She looks different in the profile picture of her account, but it's definitely her. Then, underneath that were replies, questioning why she had slept with Ila, why this was only coming out now, asking for evidence (which the girl did not have). Ila was being messaged and mentioned by what seemed to be everybody under the sun, everybody who had ever had a Twitter account, asking her if it was true, asking the girl if it was true, asking Joyce if it was true, asking the world if it was true. It was shared by trans rights people with an undeniable glee. The girl followed up that tweet with *she had a black cock strap-on, which was pretty weird anyway, it was the first red flag.*

What had she done? What had she said? The girl said she didn't want to get into details, but she had called her "a tranny," which is not a word Ila had ever used before, or ever even wanted to use. The girl tweeted that. She said *she called me a tr*nny*, asterisk and all, but then someone replied to *that* tweet telling her that even if she was censoring it, it still wasn't okay for her to use because she wasn't trans, so she deleted it. Ila couldn't keep track of anything anymore. Her high little brain was doing somersaults inside her skull. She held her finger down over the app icon for Twitter until it shook, and a small cross appeared next to it. She pressed that, and the app went grey for a moment before vanishing. But then she looked up at her laptop screen and there it was. Twitter was still open as a tab and, knowing it was a terrible idea, she clicked onto it. Somebody was alleging that *terfs* (meaning her) *actually get off on transphobia. why do so many chasers become terfs?*

Back before the House, Ila had slept with transwomen, including Alice. She had loved the idea of riding a woman's dick. But, Christ, that didn't make her a *chaser*, did it? That didn't mean anything at all, surely. She had never purposely sought out transwomen to fuck, or to fuck her. She didn't know what anything meant, and cursed herself for getting high, for ever having touched weed in the first place, you piece of shit cunt stoner, she said to herself, piece of shit cunt traumatised stoner.

She shut off the tab. If you don't look at the wound, maybe it isn't really there. Maybe that isn't blood that you feel flowing down you. And anyway, online life moved fast. Maybe by tomorrow everyone would have forgotten about who she was. Maybe they would never forget.

She pulled herself off of her bed and went to the bathroom. It hadn't been cleaned in a while. Long black hairs curled around the inside of the sink and covered the bar of soap by the shower. She didn't have a bath, just a shower. The light in the bathroom was harsh, made her look strange in the smeary mirror. Ila stared at herself through the filthy glass, asking who she was. Was she who she thought?

You want to know what happened, don't you?

What do you mean? The House was all around her. It crawled up behind her reflection in the mirror and pushed itself into the self that looked back at her through the glass. Made its eyes flicker red and its mouth twist and bubble. Is that who I am? she thought. Then again, what do you mean?

In the room. The root of everything. The heart of everything the heart of why you can't be okay. You want to know what happened to you, don't you?

I know what happened to me, she said. Alice raped me. Whatever anyone else says, I know that's true. You know that, right? You were there. We were inside you.

Yes. And Alice is out there, in the world. Carrying on.

Has she done it again?

Ila put her hand against the glass, and then brought it back and slapped it open-palmed.

Has she done it again? Has she done it to other girls? Tell me. Tell me.

The House did not answer. She removed her hand from the glass, still looking at her reflection. Then, she slapped herself on the side of the head. It was painful. Not as painful as if somebody else had done it. Your body stops you from hitting yourself that hard, but it was hard enough to hurt, hard enough to make a noise.

Come to me.

No.

Bring her to me. Come with her together arm in arm and come into my body and walk into my heart again of your own free will as you once did.

Why should I? The last time she had gone in there she had nearly died.

Because you want to move on, don't you? You want to wreak your violence on her for what she did.

I do.

You want to be okay. Think of it as a therapy. Think of it as radical.

How can I trust you?

You cannot trust a House any more than you can trust a person but think about what just became of your life, Ila, what are you going to do now, where are you going to go? They all hate you, they all think you're sick. If you stay on as you are you'll be dead in a month. By your own hand, I think. Come. Bring her. Bring yourself. Arms entwined. There is a storm coming that will swallow this country whole and all the filth within it will be drowned and washed down over the white cliffs and you don't want to be one of them do you Ila my sweet my love you want to live so come back into me bring her come back soon I miss you so much.

She looks at herself in the mirror. When the House speaks, it comes from no mouth. The voice is just there, in the absence suddenly, and then it is gone again. In the mirror Ila can see that she is a haunted house. She does not possess herself; her traumas sometimes come and peer out of the windows of her eyes and that is very frightening. I can see you there. I know you are inside. Turning over and over like a manic ballerina. On the tops of your toes until they snap audibly. I can see you, you with the nose you hate, that they used to poke with their fingernails, the other girls, the white ones, big nosed bitch, the skin you hate and that you slowly watched all the girls appropriate by colouring themselves in dark with the sun on their summer holidays, looking like plastic doll versions of you, I see you, the words all white over your skin, forming complete sentences. Panicking and screaming for help. Panicking and screaming for redemption and release.

Albion welcomes you says the House *Albion understands you* although it does not, it hates her too of course, but she's too fucked up to realise what the House really wants from her. She's desperate for something, and so this is it, that something. A cord which she can hold onto and pull on now she's drowning. Help me.

Albion is hungry and it hasn't eaten in so, so very long, and now its two girls are so ripe and fat with the red juice of potential hate. It tugs on their lifelines, and they are pulled back.

Sometimes, at the end of everything, the only option you have is to make it worse.

More than anything, and this is painful to admit but it is the truest thing: Ila misses Alice. She hates her, but she misses her. This whirl of confusion makes her miss her even more, the rock-hard sureness of holding onto her shoulders. In Ila's head Alice is sometimes barely even a person, no more than a cock in a badly fitting dress. Sometimes she is a full being, however, one with thoughts, wants, ideals, and reasons for conducting herself in the manner that she has done. Ila presses her palm into the words on her stomach, then moves it to the vague word on her thighs, *panic*, or whatever it said. She has lots of hidden meanings inscribed into her. Some kind of... government experiment, a woman covered in triggers, triggering violence and deep state decay every time she strips down, triggering sleeper cells on the beach in summer when they look with desire. A man looks at this scarred woman idly sunbathing, and suddenly he goes blank. Leaves his family there. Takes the train to London, where he hunts down an anti-racism activist and chokes her to death. It happens. You would be surprised to know how much things like that happen. The girl Ila called a tranny, the one who ran from her, hasn't felt the same since, and she didn't even focus properly on those words. That girl didn't even see the stomach scar, as it was covered by black ribbon. However, despite never seeing it, the scar often appears in her dreams, the words carved into the inside of her eyelids. And in the next general election, without even really knowing why, she votes for UKIP. She is a young, left-liberal woman. But... she wants to be able to get a good job as a nurse, and immigration means that there are less jobs to go around, especially for young working-class white women who are well educated. Is it clear how all of this works? How easy it is to slip, unthinking, into ways that the House wants you to be? Ila is a political being, with a political body, in a political situation, in a political house on a political street, in the middle of a political city, and this political city has a political history, it used to house the headquarters of the British Union of Fascists, the political city is in a political country in a political world where the bombs are always five minutes to midnight and, did you know that there are still ghettos? People still live in ghettos, not far from here. You could drive to your nearest ghetto a short while. How fucking horrifying is that. Just because Biden won in America, that doesn't mean all will be right. It's worse now than ever. Now it is time to *panic*.

Ila exits the bathroom like a ghost and picks up her phone. *I need to talk to you*, she types. *Can we please meet? In a public place? I really, really need to talk with you.*

When Ila was little, she wanted to be an archivist when she grew up. But now she's grown and the only archive she keeps is one of all the traumatic experiences she has faced, all the racist abuse on the street, all the sexual harassment and violence, carefully filed away in the back of her head.

To her surprise, Alice replies. *Okay. Meet me at Queen Park, near the dead tree.*

It's easy to forget that they really did love each other. They were thrown together by accident – Ila just happened to sit down next to Alice in a lecture, and Alice had leant over to her halfway through the lecture and, out of nowhere, commented that the lecturer looked like Steve Buscemi. Ila had started to chuckle, and found that she was completely incapable of hiding the laughter. The more her laughter echoed around the (silent) lecture hall, the harder she laughed. Alice couldn't help it either. It made no sense – it wasn't particularly funny that the lecturer looked like Steve Buscemi. And yet there they were, both girls close to tears with laughter, every eye in the cavernous room glaring at them, which only made it funnier. That was how they met, with everyone else in the room hating them. After that, they got coffee, and that was it. They fell into each other's orbit and became inseparable, and Hannah, Ila's housemate at the time, completed the trio soon after, although she never fully fit into the equation. And that was that, for quite a while. Until…

They both slept badly. When dreams came, they were jagged things, pressing themselves close until they came away bloody.

The sun is too bright for Alice, who sits on the bench she arranged to meet Ila at. It is a winter sun that blinds but doesn't warm anything at all. There's a chill wind blowing at her, nipping at her exposed skin. She's smoking her second cigarette within ten minutes and looking at two pigeons fight over a single crumb when Ila appears, ten minutes late almost exactly. They nod to each other, and Ila sits on the bench next to her, but at the furthest end, as far as she can get whilst still being on the same bench. This is the first time she's seen Alice outside of a picture or a video in three years. Alice has put on weight. Her jawline is less defined now. She looks less hot than she used to, Ila thinks, and smirks, but just as she entertains the cruel idea Alice speaks.

"How's the cancellation going?"

"I haven't been online since last night. I don't know."

"Ah, well, that TV writer is defending you, so that's something." Alice blows smoke out into the cold air.

The park they are sitting in is haunted. Specifically, there is a tree which some people call the dead tree. The strange thing about the dead tree is that it isn't actually dead at all. They can both see it from where they're sitting, it's directly opposite the bench, on the other side of a green expanse. People call it the dead tree because it looks dead, at first. It rarely produces any foliage, and yet it is still, by all accounts, a living tree. The park rangers considered cutting it down, but there was no real reason they could find to actually do that, so the tree stayed. That was lucky. If they had felled it, they would have had some sort of curse placed upon them for doing so. They would all have died in their beds, with sticks shoved deep down their throats to choke them.

A drunk died beneath the tree one night when he tried to sleep there. He was tired and a long way from home, so he settled beneath its branches, not realising where he was. Thinking himself to be safe. He awoke in the cool dark night to see something terrible in the shape of a woman framed against the moon. At first he thought it was truly a woman, and called out to it, hey love, what're you doing, or something along those lines. The thing was entirely silent, though. It shuffled towards him, getting closer and closer, blocking out the black sky and the few visible stars not blotted out with light pollution. He couldn't move, he was too drunk still, too sick and desperate. The thing that wasn't a woman was close enough to touch him, and then it did. It touched him, and it touched him hard. So hard that he died. It isn't clear how anybody knows about what the man saw. He died without telling anybody. He was completely alone in the park when the incident occurred. But people know that the tree is haunted.

People will often flock to the same places to kill themselves, the same bridges, the same woods, the same bathrooms of the same motorway service stations. Once someone kills themself in a place, it becomes hungry for more suicides. And so this was the case with the dead tree. Over its history lots of women, jilted by lovers, facing financial ruin, high on heroin, have climbed its branches and hung themselves. Or been hanged. Perhaps strung up by something, or someone. People have seen a spectre... of an elderly woman trying to cut her own throat with a straight razor, screaming silently. The ghosts in this exterior space are silent... silent women. Silent dead women. It's possible that what killed the homeless man was a spectre of one of these many female suicides, that its twisted shape was the result of a broken neck caused by hanging. It's also possible that the man simply died of a heart attack. Though that does not explain how sometimes men, standing underneath this tree, are reminded of how much of a bitch their mother was to them during their childhood, or how much they despise their ex-wives.

And the birds shun it. Right now, there are no birds at all resting on the tree's branches. Alice stares at the tree whilst talking to Ila.

"Alice," says Ila, "do you think about it?"

"About what?"

"The room."

Of course she does. "I think about it every night."

"So do I. And every day. It's like these past three years have been... just endless fallout. I thought I had made progress, started to free myself of it, of the voices and the memories and the nightmares, but it's back again, worse than before. It's the same with you, isn't it?"

"It never left with me. But yes, things have been worse lately. I thought I had burned it all away, but here you are, I guess. I can't live without you."

Today, Alice displays the cunt scar cut into her forehead proudly, for the first time ever. She rubs at it lightly, feeling like the Harry Potter of transphobic hate crime victims. "I've been thinking about getting some kind of surgery to cover this cunt up."

"I thought," says Ila snidely, "that you wanted surgery to get one." Alice ignores the comment.

"Every time I take off my clothes I see what you did." Under Ila's dress, the words throb, like they're fresh.

"Ila." Alice still isn't looking at her. She can't. "I didn't do it."

"Fuck you," Ila says, quietly. "You're fucking... trying to gaslight me, or whatever. Just like Joyce is trying to do. Trying to turn my own history against me. I know what happened. I know what happened to me. The fact that you're wearing a fucking *dress* can't change that, can it? You're racist, and you're a rapist."

"Then why did you repeat it, Ila, to that girl? Why did you do the same to her? I mean, you didn't cut her forehead, but I'm sure you wanted to. Why even text me if you're going to be like this, fuck off. I don't know why I came."

Alice stands up, turning away from Ila. The tears are hot as they stream from her eyes and grow freezing cold the longer they drip down her cheeks. Ila's crying as well. Still sitting, she reaches out her hand to Alice and grabs her arm.

"Fuck off!" Alice says, and shrugs her away.

"You don't understand," calls Ila as Alice tries to leave. "Come back, please. I can end this."

Alice stops and turns around.

"What?"

"We have to." It's hard for her to speak through the tears. "We have to go back to the House, Alice. That's why I asked you to come here."

"You're fucking insane."

"It's still there. The bones of it. They knocked down parts of it, it sat there for years. They were trying to convert it into flats, but the flats still have the same shape as the old house. It's on the same foundations. I looked it up. I looked at it, from far away. I felt it. I felt it waiting for us."

The House was still there, but it had been hurt during the attempts to convert it. How much of the internal structure of the house had been knocked away? She knew that it still lived. There was enough of it there to still have power over her. The construction of the flats had stalled a while back now. It stood there, the old House, gutted and bare, open to the elements. It stood there where the House had always stood, surrounded by trees. There had been plans to tear them down as well, but they had never come to fruition. But all the time, the possibility of someone trying again was growing. The city was expanding. It would eat up the surroundings. Soon there would be no greenery left in England's fair and pleasant land, apart from on the tops of high-rise buildings, where they put gardens to remind you of what you have lost, of what this beast of concrete and metal has consumed.

"If we just go along as we are," says Ila passionately, saying the things she thinks she has to, "then we won't ever get over it. I'll keep saying you raped me, and you'll keep saying I raped you, and we'll both keep getting too fucked up to think until one of us dies."

Alice shrugs. "So what?"

"If we go back now, we can try and... I don't know. Break the cycle."

"Why would I do that? Why would I go back there with you?"

"Whatever happened," Ila says, "it's just a fucking old house. It's not really haunted." She knows that isn't true. "Literally all that will happen is we'll go in, see what we remember, talk through our feelings or whatever, cry and hug it out if you want to. Look, if you come, I will never ever say you raped me again. You can take this as an opportunity to prove it to me, if you like. To prove that I did what you say. Otherwise..."

"You know something else, don't you?" Alice sits back down on the bench, looking into her eyes. "You're scared. And not just about the cancellation. Scared about what you're capable of."

"Something is happening," she says, very, very quietly. "Something is happening to this country, Alice."

Alice has felt it too. The tension in the air. She's seen the growing number of flags. She feels unsafe walking alone, more than she ever did before. She says that she knows.

There is a storm building here. In the hills and the cities and the towns and the villages and the red wall and the red wall inside you.

Alice and Ila sit on the bench looking at the dead tree, smoking until their throats are dry. Ila puts her hand, without thinking, on Alice's.

"Do you want to go get something to drink at least?" She's afraid of the answer either way.

"Nevertheless, even though political regimes can be overthrown, and ideologies can be criticized and disowned, behind a regime and its ideology there is always a way of thinking and feeling, a group of cultural habits, of obscure instincts and unfathomable drives. Is there still another ghost stalking Europe (not to speak of other parts of the world)?"

Umberto Eco, "Ur-Fascism"

"These days, if you say that you're English, you get thrown in jail..."

Stewart Lee

PART 2

IRREVERSIBLE DAMAGE

HOUSE

Before the House was built, it existed. The ground that they grew it on was all wrong. Far beneath the earth, corpses lay which were older than God, and so when they raised the House it was already there in a way, fully formed, ready, ravenous. No live organism can continue to exist compassionately under conditions of absolute fascism, even the birds in Italy under Mussolini were observed to take part in rallies and violence. Albion, not compassionate, not sane, stood ringed by a tangled forest, holding inside, however messily, its overpowering ideology; it had stood so for a hundred years but would only stand for one more before it entered into the long process of becoming something else, at the end of which it was hoped it would seem to all the world that it had always been that way. Within, floors crumbled, ceilings gaped open, vines choked the chimneys and the windows.

Silence lay steadily against the wood and stone of the house, and whatever walked there marched on Rome.

Now, if three girls enter a house and only two leave, who is to blame?

And if both girls tell a different story, but you read online that you have to BELIEVE WOMEN, what do you? Do you decide one is a woman and one isn't, so you can believe one of them but not the other? Do you take the side of the woman who is most like you? Or the most *intersectional* one? But one is rich, and white, and trans, and the other is rich, and Asian, and a lesbian, and cis (?), and fuck, who wins here? In the end it's so hard to choose where your sympathies settle. So, you go online and find an 'intersectionality score calculator' on the internet. You use it to try to work out who is more oppressed. According to the calculator, Alice has an intersectionality score of 44, making her more privileged than 32% of others. Who these others are is unclear. Ila, meanwhile, has a score of 64. This should mean that you sympathise more with her, but you have seen inside her head, you know the way she thinks. You wonder where Hannah would score. She comes out with a score of 25. But despite this, she never left the House, whilst the others did leave; whilst they went back to their lives, she stayed there collecting dust. And anyway, you can't trust the numbers anyway. Numbers have been known to lie. Numbers have been known to show bias, statistics often have racist undertones, for example. So, there's just two girls leaving a house and maybe you don't have to take a side, maybe you can empathise with them both and hope they get the therapy and help they need and can learn to forgive one another. No. You can't do that. Are you a fucking idiot? Are you that fucking stupid that you genuinely think you can do that and that something like that is possible?

There is no electricity in the House. No generator that works, not now, not in the modern day. But even so, very occasionally, maybe once every few years, there is a faint light in one of the windows on the first floor. The light isn't coming from that room. It is too faint for that. But that room's door has been left open, and somewhere within the House, impossibly, there is a light that has been turned on. A faint, red light.

Here is a thing that happened in the House, back when England was still for the English: there was a man. Imagine him. He brought his wife with him to live there, in the House. When he purchased it, it was a corpse, as it is now, when Alice and Ila are sitting together considering the possibility of returning. He got it cheaply, but he had grand dreams of what he might turn it into, with his new wife at his side like a faithful spaniel.

The House has not read "Bluebeard", nor had the story recounted to it. The House doesn't read at all. It is not aware of the story's long shadow, of the myriad interpretations of it, mostly famously Angela Carter's "The Bloody Chamber" which transports the story into a violent feminist revenge story. The title is a simple pun, referring both to the room to which its heroine must not venture, and her pussy, bleeding after being fucked roughly by her new husband. The House doesn't know that story. But it knows this one; the one about the man who purchased it, and the wife he brought to live there. And so now sit still, because the House will tell it to you as best it can...

The man's name was Edmund. He appeared as a man named Edmund might – shorter than he wished, with his hair slicked down and a conspicuous lack of facial hair. Edmund had just returned from war and was awash with the glory of violence and victory. His father was a society man in London, and one of his father's neighbours, a lady of some quality, had two rather beautiful daughters who were in desperate need of a husband, lest they grow wrinkled and saggy before anybody snatched them up. Edmund couldn't believe anybody hadn't proposed to either of them already (they were beautiful girls!) but Edmund's father told him the reason why they remained unmarried: one of the girls' virginity was not intact, and the other was overly wilful, with ideas far beyond the station that a young woman held. Still, Edmund's father said he should consider them. The pairing of their families may be virtuous, even if the girls were not. So he met with both of them. The girl who was wilful was seventeen years old. She spent one afternoon with Edmund and vowed to never speak to him again, although when her mother asked why, she would only say that the young man was *disquieting*.

"You are too wilful, far too wilful," said her mother. "I fear no man will ever want you." But that was just how the girl liked it, so she smiled to herself.

The second girl, the one who was not a virgin, was called Emily. She was a little older than her sister, which Edmund disliked. However, she enjoyed Edmund's presence and he found that he enjoyed her presence in turn, despite her lack of honour. After meeting him, she told her mother that yes, she would be happy to marry him. Her mother was overjoyed. Edmund's father was, too, thinking of those piles of capital that would soon exchange hands. But Edmund and his bride-to-be would need a place to live, and Edmund asked, might they take a place away from the city. He had been at war, and he tired of the noise of London, the curling filth of the smogs. His father grumbled at the idea, but agreed to help him buy a place, and this was how Edmund came into possession of the House.

Edmund was insulted when he first actually set eyes on the House. Was this what his father thought of him?

"They call it Albion," said the man he had hired to head the desperately-needed building work.

"Albion?" asked Edmund. It was a queer name for a house, but he liked how it felt in his mouth. Not Albion Hall, or Albion House. Just Albion. The Giant, the mythical founder of Britain, who lived and died in its luscious green hills. His body was buried off the southern coast of England, in a circle of trees, a colossal corpse on the top of which sprouted a fertile forest.

The name was kept. The building work took a year, a year in which Edmund stayed in London and wedded Emily.

"Oh," he said, whilst fucking her in their marital bed, "when I take you to Albion it shall be like a second wedding night."

She lay beneath him, her legs spread. His sweat dripped from his face down into her open mouth. While they lived in London, Albion took shape. Its walls remained the same, but the insides were pulped and moulded to fit the current fashions. And, when it was done, a small fleet of meek servants were hired to staff the place. At this point, Edmund and Emily left their London lodgings and travelled down south, eagerly awaiting the first sight of the House.

And it was impressive. Edmund had only ever lived in London, and, however nice those city houses, they were nothing compared to a true, traditional country house. Not quite as big as the old ones, of course. They sprawled over acres of land, whereas Albion was really just one building, a dark cube of stone. But the servants put on such a show of a welcome, with all the lights burning on, and they stood out in front of the door to bring the married couple into their new home. Emily was surprised at how big it all was. Like Edmund, she had always been a city girl, but the moment she stepped through those front doors she was nearly shocked out of her skin at the entrance hall, which stretched upwards from the floor all the way to the very top of the house, a great mouth covered in varnished wood. And the staircase, a tongue, which Edmund carried her up two steps at a time. She was terrified he would drop her.

There was a great dining room, and kitchens, and everything she could have ever wanted. And so many rooms... more rooms than she would ever need.

As the two of them ran from room to room, laughing at this newfound space, one of the servants turned to the other.

"I wonder if they know," she said, under her breath, "what happened to the last man to own this house?"

"Or," murmured the other, "what happened to his wife. Wonder if they'd be laughin' like that if they did."

They were happy, the married couple. That first night in Albion really was like a second wedding night. For Emily it felt like losing her virginity all over again, but she did not vocalise this thought. The sheets on the bed were softer than they had been in London. The curtains that hung all around it allowed them to play sensual games with one another, looking at the others' silhouette through the fabric. The whole place was stunning. The surrounding countryside was beautiful and Edmund, who owned an automobile, would drive as fast as he could around the hairpin bends, his wife holding onto anything she could out of panic.

It did not take long for Edmund to find out the true nature of Albion's origins, which his father had kept from him. Sometimes men would make comments at him, saying that he lived in a house built for a deviant, to which he often became very angry, throwing glasses at the wall and shouting at whoever had said it that he was the one who fucking made this house, he had built it, not some other man. This wasn't true. He hadn't ever built anything in his life. He wouldn't know how. These violent moments scared Emily. They were a side of her husband she did not know how to deal with. When he was like this, she thought that maybe she had made some deep, terrible mistake.

But she loved him anyway.

As their marriage grew in love and complexity, so Albion grew around them. The servants grew to dislike the House, but they could never articulate why. If somebody asked if it was haunted, which they did, because it had been an abandoned house in which a death had occurred, they couldn't exactly say that it was. Nobody ever experienced any sort of ghostly comings and goings. But they felt that the House looked down on them, disliking their presence. It was a spiteful place. It still is. It always will be.

Edmund's name grew in stature as he started to invite guests to the house, often with very little notice, which could be taxing for both the staff and for Emily. He cultivated friendships, as best he could, using his father's name well, with politicians and scientists, criminologists, psychologists. After a year or two, he began to read, voraciously, writings about race and racial difference, about sex. About, more than anything else, eugenics. This started as a simple academic interest, but Emily watched, with helpless curiosity, as it grew and grew in intensity. After two years it had gone from perusing books and inviting authors for dinners (which Emily would have to sit through, ignored), to a very real passion. He began talking about wishing to investigate the matter *practically* despite the fact that he had no background in the sciences at all. Emily did not know what he meant by *practically*, not at first. Not until that day.

He had been in London on "business," leaving Emily to wander the empty halls of Albion on her own, lonely and bored. They had started to fill them out with furnishings and paintings but neither of them had much of a taste for the arts, and she often found that, once something was installed, it didn't match anything else. This aggravated her. It made her eyes sore. She was in a mood when he returned from his business trip. Happy to finally have him back, she ran from the room and to the first-floor landing, looking down the stairs to see him. Only then she found that he had not returned home alone. He had a black woman with him. She stood next to him at the foot of the stairs, gazing around in wonder at the interior of the House. The woman's name was Agatha, although neither Edmund nor Emily ever asked for her name. He had approached her on the streets of London, and she had expected that he wished to pay her for sex, when suddenly he offered an extortionate amount to accompany him back to his home. She was in no position to refuse payment of that level, no matter if the request made her suspicious. And it made her very, very suspicious. The moment she had gotten into the carriage with him, she had regretted this – no amount of money was worth dying for, she thought, and she kept thinking it all the way down the long road to Albion. At any moment she expected the carriage to stop, and when it did, he would take her out into the fields of the woods and have her and leave her there, dead or dying. It happens. It had happened to girls she'd known. But he had taken her all the way, and here she was, in the mouth of Albion, with Emily standing at the top of the stairs glaring at her with horror. Who was this, who her husband had brought here? She was possessed of a violent jealousy as she watched her husband lead her up the stairs towards her.

As they passed, Edmund looked at Emily very seriously.

"Now, my beloved wife, I am going to take this individual here into my study. Don't disturb me, even if it is time to eat. I will eat when I please. Take your dinner without me if you must. Whatever you do, do not disturb my work."

Edmund's study was on the first floor. It was at the end of a long corridor. Just when you thought the corridor was far too long, unnaturally so, that was where the study was. At the very end. It was the one room in the house that Emily was forbidden to enter. A man must have his own, private, space, said Edmund. In fact, he told her that if she ever entered the room without his express permission that he would beat her, and beat her *hard*. So, she didn't disturb him. She knew she mustn't. But, God, the jealousy she felt, watching that woman, that woman whom she considered clearly lesser than herself in every manner, being taken into Edmund's study when she, herself, his very own wife, was not permitted to see it. That jealousy was very nearly overwhelming. She spent the entire evening waiting around the downstairs of the house, listening carefully for some noise from upstairs. When Edmund came out, the staff served dinner for them both, and the married couple sat and ate. Agatha, the woman Edmund had taken into the room with him, had not come back out at the same time. Emily wondered if she should ask what had happened to her, where she had gone, but found she was too frightened. The woman must simply have slipped away, she thought. Somehow.

This was not the last time Edmund brought back a 'guest'. Every few months, he would go away for a few days and return with one in tow. They were usually women, and usually not white. Emily learned to let him have this quirk, however much it ate at her.

One time, he brought a white woman with him. Emily was stunned by this – this was something different. She was very beautiful, very tall and slender, with bright blue eyes. The jealousy was there again, filling her entire body. She clenched her fists as she listened to the two of them ascending the stairs. Again, though, Edmund came back out of his study, but the lady did not.

This time, Emily felt brave enough to ask him. She steeled herself and said, "That woman... who was she? Where did she go?"

He was silent, and she was sure she had crossed a line. But then he spoke: "That, my dear," he said, "was not a woman."

"But Edmund, I saw her!"

"I found... it... in Bristol. Pretending to everybody around him that he was a woman. And he put on quite the performance, you know. Nearly had me fooled, too. But I found him fascinating, you know, he had received some sort of rudimentary surgery? He had lost his manhood, as it were."

Emily blushed. "And what happened to him? I did not see him leave."

Edmund shrugged. "Oh, don't you worry, my pretty dear. Don't you worry at all."

The door to Edmund's study was painted black, and had a small, gold keyhole. Emily had, of course, tried to look through that keyhole, but found that nothing was visible through it at all. All that she could see was an intense liquid red colour. It must be from the wallpaper, she thought. Emily did have access to the key. He had even told her which key would open the study – it was a small, gold one. But she was a good wife, and she wished to do what he asked. But this became increasingly difficult, as he brought more and more of these unsavoury guests back from his trips. With each *thing* he brought into her house, her curiosity grew, and her violent jealousy. She did not only wonder too hard and too long about why these guests never seemed to reappear, but about what Edmund did to them in that red room. She would lie awake in bed next to him, vividly fantasising about her husband treating her like some kind of scientific object, to be studied, to be used and discarded.

Edmund grew increasingly frustrated with her. Their marriage was not the haven he had hoped. No matter how much he fucked her, she seemed incapable of producing a baby. She tried every method she could think of, and nothing worked.

"I need a son!" he screamed at her. "I should have forced your sister to marry me! She would have given me five sons by now, at least!"

Emily cried at his words. He looked at her. She was a pathetic specimen. He threw his glass at her head, and she only just managed to duck. It shattered against the wall, the dark brown alcohol staining the paper. And however much he shouted, however much he began to threaten physical harm, no baby came. She wondered if losing her virginity outside of marriage had cursed her. He took to calling her slutwife.

When he arrived home, with one of his guests, he would greet her: *hello, dear slutwife. Do not disturb me, lovely slutwife.*

He spent increasing amounts of time in his study, alone. The frequency of his guests grew, too, as did his trips elsewhere, to London, to Bristol, and abroad, to Paris, to Berlin. It was whilst he was on one such trip that Emily broke. She couldn't bear it anymore. The marriage was coming apart all around her, at its very centre, its very foundations, perhaps. This room, from which she was forbidden. These activities, which were reserved for others and never for her. Why did he like all these others so much more than her? Did he fuck them, and, if he did, did they ever become pregnant with his illegitimate children? She strode up the stairs and down that endless corridor, walking with purpose towards Edmund's room. The key, small and bright, was between her thumb and forefinger. It slipped with ease into the lock and turned. Her heart was thumping about inside her, like a drum beating her head, screaming *what are you doing, oh, Emily, what are you doing, what have you done?*

Yet there was another voice, a voice without and within. *Emily look inside* it said.

The door opened. She was ready, craving answers. I know you are, too. You want to know what was inside. Women hung from hooks like slaughtered pigs. Corpses preserved in glass. But no. She saw none of that at all. What she saw was, in a way, even stranger. It was, quite simply, Edmund's study. The walls were papered with a vivid red, devoid of any pattern. The only piece of furniture was a desk, pushed against the far wall. The floor was wooden and bare. There was a single light in the ceiling. It was a bare, disappointing room, but one she felt compelled to enter. Her footsteps *click-clacked* across the floorboards as she walked over to the desk, in the far corner. On top of it were a series of tools – a pair of calipers, a scalpel, a bone saw and some rope. She opened the drawers of the desk, but the only items in them were financial papers, letters from Edmund's bank and so on. She backed away. There was one more thing of note in the room: opposite where the desk was pushed, there was a second door. She went to it, but it was locked tightly. It did not even have a keyhole. However Edmund had locked it, there was no way of bypassing it, not without kicking the door down, and Emily was certainly not about to start doing that. Emily's heart sank with disappointment. Her husband's bloody chamber was empty. It was a room with nothing in it. No fresh gore. She wasn't sure what she had wanted to see, but it hadn't been this.

She left the room, and locked the door behind her, but to her horror found that the key had been stained red by the lock – what she had seen through the keyhole hadn't been the red wallpaper at all, it had been ink. Edmund had contrived to put red ink in the keyhole, so that her copy of the key would show that she had broken her promise not to enter the room. She ran to the bathroom, but no amount of soap and warm water would remove the ink from the little gold key. While she was still trying her best to fruitlessly wash away the blood-red ink, she heard the front door open, and Edmund called out that he was home.

"My dear," he said as she walked down the stairs. He had a guest – an Indian girl. She looked no more than twelve. The girl's eyes were fixed on the carpet and her head was bowed. She knew her place, thought Emily. Edmund, of course, had his own key to the room. She didn't need to worry about him seeing what she had done to her copy. He took his guest upstairs, and she waited a few minutes before she followed them. While he worked, she sat down on the floor outside of the room, listening as best she could to what went on in there, although the noises were indistinct. She pressed her ear up close to the door and strained hard, but all she could hear was her husband's feet, *click-clacking* on the floor.

The next day, Edmund came to her. "My dear," he asked, "I seem to have misplaced the key to the basement. Might I use yours?"

"Of course," she said. Emily ran to her room, sweating heavily, and removed the basement key from the ring. Whatever happened, she couldn't let him know that she had been in his study. However, when she brought the basement key to him, he asked the question she dreaded to hear.

"Dear, might I see your copy of the key to my study?"

She gulped. "Why would you need to do that?"

It was obvious, of course, that he somehow knew she had been in his room. Or at least, that he suspected, and now sought to confirm his suspicion.

He simply smiled in response.

"You know, Edmund," she said, tiptoeing with her words. "I fear I must have misplaced it."

He stared at her strangely. "Well," he said, after a few seconds of silence. "We can't have that, can we. Come, we shall look in the bedroom for it. I'm sure it simply slipped off the ring."

She followed him, mutely, considering if it would be possible to make any kind of escape. But why? She loved Edmund, even as she felt endless sadness that she was, apparently, barren and useless to him. She did not want to run. He had told her that he would beat her if she entered his study, yes, so she would take the beating like she took the beatings from her mother. Emily was not a coward. She was an Englishwoman, of English blood.

The ring of keys was laying on her dressing table. Edmund lifted them up, jingling them, and inspecting each in turn until he came to the last key, the golden key, now caked in red ink. Emily tried her best not to start crying.

"Emily," he said, "I told you that if you entered my study, I would beat you."

Her face was red as she tried to screw her eyes shut, so that the tears might now come. She nodded.

"Why did you do it?"

"I–" she said breathlessly, "—I had to know. All those women, Edmund. You spend so much time with them, and not with me. Your wife. What do they have, that I do not?"

He laughed, then. "Oh, my poor little jealous wife! I can't beat you for that, dear. You want to know what I do in my room, to all those guests I have? Fine. I will show you. I will do the same to you."

He led her to the room, walking slowly. She could have run there, she was so anxious, confused and eager like a little puppy. He opened the door with her copy of the key. The room was the same as it had been when she had entered like a thief in the night. He lay her down on the wooden floor, beneath that single, burning light on the ceiling. She felt the room began to throb around her, like it was coming alive. He locked the door behind them. He tied first her wrists together, then her ankles. He produced a piece of cloth from one of the pockets of his suit and made her lift her head up off of the floor so that he could loop it around her mouth to gag her. She was a good little wife to him. Rarely did she ask for anything, apart from that one single transgression. Well, that and the desert of her womb.

And suddenly, the room went completely silent. She stared up into the light in the ceiling, even though it burned her eyes. Had Edmund left the room? She couldn't hear him, but she didn't want to look. If she looked, she thought, she would be doomed. She shut her eyes instead, but the burning white light remained even through her eyelids. There was no sound of Edmund's presence, no breathing from him or even *click-clacking* footsteps. Everything was silent.

At the last moment, she realised that she did not, in fact, want to know what had happened to all of those other women. Scores of them, over the time they had lived there. Countless amounts, led into this very position, never to return, not once. If this was a jest, a punishment, a sexual act, even, she would very much like it to stop. Emily was frightened. The most frightened she had ever felt. She opened up her eyes again, and began to try to scream, but the gag was tied too tight around her mouth to even breathe properly, let alone cry for help. Her eyes registered something undefinable. It blotted out the light that shone down hot from above her, it cast a shadow across her face. Was it Edmund? It was dark and faceless and red, the red of it dripping all around her, filling up her eyes and her mouth, investigating between her legs, pushing into her, waves of red flowing up inside her cunt like cum, but so much more cum than could ever have been produced by a man, ballooning her useless womb until it was ready to burst inside of her. Red tore the fabric of the gag and slid down her throat, into her lungs and her stomach. Albion reached inside her, all around her, nestled against her, gnashed its teeth and ripped at her flesh. *You're useless, you're useless, you're fucking useless*, it screamed close in her ears, so she could feel its hot breath against her skin. This was what happened. That was what it felt like.

They found Emily's body a week later beneath one of the pine trees near the house. Her womb and vagina had been surgically removed, although where the organs had gone was not clear. The servants knew nothing at all. She had been there one day, they said, and then she was gone. The Master had said nothing of it. When they arrested Edmund and questioned him on the matter, he refused to say anything at all, other than admitting that yes, he had killed her, and that he would very much like to be hanged by the neck until he was dead.

HANNAH

Hannah got to the bar with a full half hour to go before her date was supposed to arrive and she felt like kicking herself for it. This always happened. It was always this; that she got there far too early and had to stand around jiggling her leg until the time she was actually meant to be there, or she'd turn up late, sweating and out of breath. Some fairy had cursed her in childhood, she guessed, with some archaic riddle that meant *you shall always be early or late but never on time.* Being early meant you got drunk first. It meant everyone else had to play catch up to you, and you felt like an alcoholic because you were still going, even as they did shots to get to your level. Despite this, she got a drink and sat at a waxy-feeling wooden table that was right up against one of the glass windows that looked out onto the street, where it was just starting to drizzle. She sat, leaning against the window and sipped her rum and coke. *God you dumb bitch*, she thought to herself, not unkindly, *arriving early like this and now everyone in the bar thinks you're a loner.* By the time her date arrived, she might well have finished this drink and be onto her second one. What would he think of her, when he turned up and she was already drunk?

Her phone buzzed lowly. Alice had texted her, wishing her luck and reminding her not to do anything *she* wouldn't. Hannah replied, *I can do basically anything, then?*

Alice and Ila had wanted to come on the date. When she'd told them, playfully but firmly, to fuck off, they'd asked if they could at least be in the bar, maybe sat on the other side just to make sure she was safe.

"I'm an adult!" she'd said. "What on earth is your problem, god. I've gone on a hundred dates with boys before."

Ila shrugged. "I just don't trust men."

"Alice fucks thousands of men!"

Alice looked offended. "Thousands? I think you're probably overestimating a bit there."

"You get what I mean."

The maternalistic worrying had made Hannah feel worse than she expected. She'd stormed out, not looking at either of them, or caring enough to say goodbye. They were jealous. It was very clear. She didn't know why, but they were always, always jealous, and that jealousy was projected onto her. She sometimes thought they resented her for not being into women, for being unable to fully form the third corner of their triangle, for throwing off the balance and rejecting their free love. But at the same time as these thoughts occurred, she worried that she was being homophobic, reading into things that were never there. The only thing she was sure of was that it hurt. And the thing that made it worse was that, if they had said nothing she would have been perfectly fine, but, thanks to their worrying, they had put the idea in her head that there really was something unsafe about the whole thing. It was just a simple, straightforward Tinder date with a guy she found attractive. But maybe they did know best, after all.

The bar was full and bright. It had signs in the women's toilets telling her that if she felt uncomfortable, all she had to do was Ask for Angela at the bar and someone would get her some help. It was safe here. But, what, said her mind, if it *wasn't*?

She finished the drink and ordered another. Her head was pressed against the window. The glass felt cold and refreshing, and as she looked out onto the street, she saw him. Her date. He walked past, not looking to his left, and then there he was again framed in the yellow light in the bar's entrance, slowly pulling his scarf from around his neck. His eyes darted around the bar, looking for a face he recognised. He almost missed her, his eyes went right past her and then backtracked, settling, and the sides of them creased with a smile.

Brandon walked over to her table. Hannah thought he looked better than his profile had made him seem, which was often the case with men – men don't know how to take pictures of themselves, or how to present themselves in a way that is attractive, making it hard to work out who is actually hot and who isn't. But here he was, and it was certain that he was definitely hot. Brandon was tall and black and shockingly handsome. Her insides twitched as he edged between the tables towards her. She nearly forgot to stand up. She kissed his cheek. His skin was soft. At that moment she was already certain she wanted him inside her.

"So, Hannah, what do you study?" he asked.

Hannah was looking at him with wide-eyes, and realised that he had spoken, but she hadn't been listening.

"I'm sorry," she said. "What did you say again?"

Alice didn't like Brandon.

"But *why?*" demanded Hannah, as they sat around in front of their textbooks, trying, and failing, to do some kind of studying. It was the last term at university, the end of their three years as one cohesive trio. They all had futures to head to, postgraduate courses in other cities that, of course, they wouldn't end up ever doing. But at the time, this was the thought: this is going to be our last summer together, and we are going to make it count.

"I just, I don't know. He seems too good to be true, doesn't he, Ila?" Alice was begging for some kind of back-up.

Ila shrugged. "I don't like men," was all she said, "and he's a man."

At the same bar where Hannah and Brandon had their first date, they were all getting drunk together to celebrate handing in their final pieces. Hannah technically had a week's extension, but she wanted to be there, and Brandon was there, too. They could only get a table with four chairs because the whole place was packed, so Hannah sat on Brandon's lap, feeling his warm arms loop around her front like a protective harness. Hannah wanted the tension gone. She wanted them to be friends, just for this summer, before the group dissolved and each of them went into the future. And they seemed to be getting on just fine. Even Ila, sceptical as she was of men, was enjoying herself, talking to Brandon about Audre Lorde. Hannah couldn't follow the conversation, but she enjoyed sitting there anyway, hearing the discussion flow around her. Alice sat, quiet, next to Ila. She didn't see anything at all.

When Hannah went home with Brandon that night, he asked the question she'd dreaded. What was Alice's problem with him? Was she racist? Was she jealous? Or was it his fault, had he said something offensive without realising, and if so, was there anything he could do to apologise? Hannah appreciated the care and the concern, but she had to break it to him that the answer was, quite simply, she had no idea why Alice seemed to hate him, or why she had even come at all that night if she did.

Deep in the summer now. They were cuddling around a fire on the beach, sweating after the exertion of the Pride Parade, drinking endless, lethal amounts of Buckfast from a glass bottle. The fire they made on the stones was hypnotic. As Hannah lay there watching it, she felt herself drifting off to sleep. When she woke, she could feel something press against her. She stayed silent. The air was full of the sounds of hundreds of people just like them, calling out to the sea. The fire had gone low and was now only embers. Whatever it was that pressed against her back did so again, and she hurried a glance out of the corner of her eye. Ila was on top of Alice, out there for anyone to see, riding her. Ila threw her head back in rapture. Hannah screwed her eyes shut tightly and tried, as hard as she could, to go back to sleep.

"It's fucking ridiculous."

Alice was trying to focus on the boiling pasta in front of her, but she was failing completely.

"You know how many homeless people there are in this city?"

Hannah shrugged. "I have no idea."

Alice didn't give an answer to her own question, she just kept ranting.

"And there's buildings just sitting there, hoarded by fucking property developers. You know that house out on Station Road, the one that has its back to the woods?"

Of course she knew it. She hadn't grown up in the city, she'd only moved here for university, but even then it had become part of the city's lore for her. The shadowy rectangle of old stone which even the local teenagers feared. They had a game, apparently. They liked to see how close they could get before they had to turn back. There were no genuine stories of ghosts, or murders, or the sort of bloody tales that keep places like that abandoned and let them drop into the realm of popular myth, but it still occupied the space of a place where those things had occurred. The house. The House.

"So what?" asked Ila.

"You ever been there?"

The pasta was nearly boiling over, but it wasn't even done. Alice turned down the hob as much as she could. They were in Ila's flat, which sucked, but it had a kitchen big enough for the three of them to fit into.

"I've walked up to the door. Got as far as putting my hand on it. But I didn't go in."

"Why?"

"It's haunted" she said. "I don't believe in ghosts but still, fuck, that place felt so... wrong."

Alice did believe in ghosts, but she let herself get worked up about this.

"Is it, or is that what they want you to think?"

"Who?"

"The people that own it. See, if it didn't have a reputation, it would be harder for them to keep. People would break in there to squat. There'd be pressure to turn it into public housing. But as it is, no, they can't do that, because it's haunted, because it's cursed. I guarantee you, the origin of all those stories is the property developers who are waiting it out."

Ila wasn't convinced. "But I felt it."

"You'd been told you should feel it, so you did."

"I'm surprised," said Hannah. "You told me you've seen ghosts before."

"I believe in ghosts." Alice strained the pasta, which steamed up, the hot water vapour curling in the air. "I don't believe in haunted houses."

There's a difference between a ghost story and a haunted house story. This feels so basic, but also so hard to articulate. A ghost story is about the thing that it tells you it is about: a ghost, an ephemeral thing from beyond the grave, trying to contact the living. A haunted house story is about more than that. It is about structure, architecture, and history. Like Jamaica Inn, a haunted house that isn't haunted at all, but people said it was to cover up the truth of the matter. There aren't any ghosts in the House. And yet it continues to be haunted despite this fact.

So it was Alice's idea to go into the house, all three of them, together, as one last hurrah, one last thing to cement their friendship before she left for Bristol, before Ila went to Edinburgh, before Hannah went back home. Hannah asked if Brandon could join them, but she knew that Alice would say no, it had to be just them. Ila was reluctant at first. She alone had been to the House before and knew how it felt. But Alice convinced her. They didn't think she heard, but Hannah knew that Alice promised to fuck her in there, amongst the spiderwebs and the dust and the rotting wood, and that had been enough. The thrill of breaking and entering, the joy of making a political statement by doing so. They didn't take sleeping bags with them, but Hannah had a thermos in her rucksack filled with hot chocolate. The plan wasn't to sleep. They would simply go in, explore, and then settle in a room together. At some point, Hannah guessed, they would vanish off, leaving her alone in the dark, before returning, hot and sweaty and unable to say what they had been doing.

It was the end of summer when they went. Hannah didn't tell her boyfriend what they were doing, because she knew he would tell her to stop, and he would be right to. It was unsafe. A deeply stupid, dangerous idea. All sorts of things could happen; the cops could come, there could be some kind of accident. These old buildings have signs outside saying that they're unsafe for a reason. But she went anyway, because she loved her friends, and she knew she would regret not going in the future.

They got the bus out halfway down Station Road, and then left it at a stop that nobody ever uses. The bus driver nodded at them, a little confused, but who is he to question what people do? The moon was up that night, a slim bright wound in the black sky hanging between the tower block and the House. They couldn't see the House yet. Not even with the lights from the tower block and from the moon. Its invisibility felt curious, and conspicuous. Alice already had her torch out, and, between the streetlights, it carved a path for them to follow in white light along the grassy bank of the roadside. Hannah walked a little behind the others. They always forgot that her being shorter meant that she couldn't keep up with them, one stride of theirs felt like it took two of hers. It was fucking annoying, in all honesty. Inconsiderate. She always ended up being the odd one out, the third wheel, even if they insisted they were only friends or whatever.

As they approached the House, she started to feel something around her. Two opposing forces, one pushing her away, and the other drawing her in. Her body couldn't decide what it wanted to do. She didn't ask if the others felt the same way, because she didn't want them to think she was weak. But they felt it too, in their own ways.

Leave here now, and then *Come closer*.

It was still hard to see, even when they got to the gates that marked the boundaries of the land. They were overgrown with vines that twisted up the rusted metal. A sign telling them to KEEP OUT hung on the gates, another saying DANGER OF DEATH placed next to it. The gates were difficult to open, the hinges had rusted shut over the years and fused together. But further along the road, along the high wall that the vines had reclaimed, they found a crumbled hole between the bricks which was big enough for a human to enter. It was easier for Hannah to get through given how small she was, so she went first, squeezing through the gap, and when she was on the other side she helped pull the others through. Ila got a graze from the stone on her upper arm and grumbled all the way up the drive to the House's front door. The drive wasn't really a drive anymore. They could still barely see anything outside of Alice's torch beam, but the light found the impression of a track leading forwards, and then settled on the door, which was old wood. Over the years the paint had chipped off, and now it was bare, and hanging open, ready to enter. Alice moved the torch across the front of the place, taking in the plants which crept up its brickwork, the windows with no glass in them. Nobody had ever bothered to board them up, so they were holes open to the elements. Even if the front door had been impossible to go through, they could have climbed into one of the windows on the ground floor easily, brushing the ivy out of the way and jumping down into the dark oblivion within. As it was, all they needed to do was push through the open door.

Alice went first, holding the torch. Hannah watched, the last of the three, as Alice edged her way inside, illuminating whatever she saw in front of her. When she was in, it was like she'd suddenly vanished completely. Hannah couldn't see her through the crack, couldn't even see the torch's light. *This is a terrible idea*, she told herself. *You could just turn back and they probably wouldn't miss you, right?*

Then Alice called for them.

"Come on!" she said, her voice distant. "It's so fucking cool in here, you have to see."

Ila was next. She put her hand on the door, as she had done when she was just a teenager and had been dared to get as close as she could. Ila had won that game. It had been a badge of pride where one was sorely needed. Now she would elbow her way past that and see what came after. She ducked down and went into the dark.

Hannah walked forwards and waited for a moment. She really could have turned back. The feeling was strong, overpowering the other feeling that tried to pull her inside. It was about to win, when Ila's hand suddenly appeared, beckoning for her to grab it. Hannah did so, and in she went.

As she went through the door, a cobweb, which somehow hadn't gotten Ila or Alice, became entangled in her hair, and she yelped, stumbled, and fell out of Ila's grasp. She hit something hard. Alice shone the light on her and laughed, as she lay there on her knees trying to pull the web out of her hair.

"Fuck you," she said.

"Are you scared?" asked Ila, who was, of course, terrified.

"Yes. Yes I'm scared."

She stood up and grasped the shoulder strap of her bag with one hand. It felt good to hold onto something, gripping it hard enough to be slightly painful.

Alice played the torchlight around the entrance hall, trying to grasp the geography of the place, which wasn't easy. The torch's beam was too small to truly see anything. In the House it was a murky, inky dark that swallowed the beam, but they could see open doorways to either side, and the staircase, desperately unsafe, sloping upwards before them. Alice turned around, and shone the light through the windows, which were thick with vegetation, so thick that the light wouldn't have been visible to anybody standing outside, looking at the building. The floorboards creaked as they moved around. Everything that wasn't them was as still as a painting.

And there were things in there with them. The House had been open for a very, very long time, and all sorts of life had found its way inside. The ivy and vines that covered the brickworks snaked around through the windows, covering the brickwork with a thick bed of tangled, knotted root. Rats scurried in the corners. Foxes nested beneath the sink in the kitchens. The house was its own habitat.

Things lived in the House, yes. But as they stood there, with the stairs in front of them, beckoning, everything was very, very still.

"Come on!" shouted Alice.

Hannah jumped as the quiet was snapped open violently. Alice was striding to the left.

"Let's look down here, find the dining room."

"How do you know the dining room is that way?" Ila called after her, hurrying.

"I don't!"

Hannah didn't want to be left there, alone, with no light at all, so she went as fast as she could after them, through a doorway that had no door. There *was* a dining room there, almost as cavernous as the entrance hall. Or at least, she thought that must be what it was. There was no table in the room, no furnishings at all. There was a hole in the middle of the floorboards, and when Alice shone the torch down it they could only see a thick layer of spiderwebs.

"We should have all brought torches," Hannah said, speaking to herself.

"Nah." Alice was putting on a confident, cavalier attitude. "This way we can't just go wandering off. We have to stick together."

"I think you just like being the one in control," murmured Ila.

It felt weird to speak loudly in the House. It felt as if they would have been breaking a taboo. Alice wanted to explore the kitchens, but the hallway that led there was impassable. The floorboards had rotted away, and parts of the ceiling had fallen in. Alice was disappointed, and worried this meant that anything on the first floor would be impossible to explore as well. She strode back out of the dining room, leaving the other two to hurry after her, both of them fearful of what it would mean to be stuck there without any light to guide them. They really, really should have brought more torches, or a lamp, or something. They got back to the entrance hall, and Alice was already halfway up the stairs.

"Shit!" called Ila, behind her.

Alice stopped. "What?"

"The stairs. Are they safe?"

Alice thought, and then jumped up, twice, on the stair she stood on. It creaked, and Hannah was sure it was going to collapse in, swallowing Alice whole. But it stayed.

"Don't be silly," she said, and kept walking up, leaving Ila and Hannah no choice but to go after her.

The stairs felt dangerously unsteady beneath her feet. *They are going to break, they are going to break*, the thought rattled inside her with every heartbeat. *They are going to break and that'll be it.* She put her hand out to grab the handrail of the stairs, and then felt a splinter of wood push its way into her palm.

"Shit. Shitshitshit." She stumbled up the last of the stairs. Alice settled the light on her. "What's wrong?"

"Fucking," she held out her hand, "fucking splinter."

She pulled it out, feeling the pain spike and then dull once the wood was gone. It wasn't a big wound, and it stopped bleeding quickly, but she was uncomfortably aware, now, of her own hand, and the feeling of the blood pumping through her. And the spot of bright, wet red glimmered in the torch-light. The House watched the three girls, and a thin line of water dripped from the ceiling. If it had been raining that night, it could have just been rain. But it wasn't. It was dry outside. The House was salivating.

There were doorways, growing out from the landing they stood on, as organised and logical as the ivy that covered the walls. Alice let the torch beam settle on each and every doorway, before moving to the next. Each one was open, with no door and no sign that there had ever been one, although there must have been. The light reached a short way down, illuminating floorboards, walls, ceilings. They were identical. Each and every corridor. Alice chose, apparently randomly. If she had some way of truly deciding, she had not consulted the others. So they went down the corridor to the left of them. It was just as good as any of the others. The only sounds were their breaths, and their feet on the floor, and the creaking of the wood as they stepped on it.

The light played over the wallpaper on each side of them, and Hannah realised that there were signs that people *had* been in here, which surprised her. And then she chastised herself for even being surprised. Of course, a great big abandoned building would have had people break inside, just like they had. And whoever had come here had left evidence of their presence. The wallpaper was rotting away, but on the pieces which remained, and on the brickwork beneath it, people had carved things in crude, jagged hands. Dicks, of course. Dicks in a variety of situations. Hannah passed dicks spewing cum out from their tips, dicks poking into assholes and cunts, dicks going into mouths, dicks going into the bodies of girls, girls with Xs over their eyes. There were double lightning bolts, some of them so large they reached from the floor to the ceiling. And there were swastikas, some of which had been aborted halfway through, some fully formed. It wasn't just like this on the walls. The wooden floors beneath them, which might, once, have been covered in carpet, were covered in words, some of them old, some of them new. She tried to read them as the three girls stopped to inspect the corridors, which had split into two. While Ila and Alice argued under their breath about which direction they should head in, Hannah dropped down to the floor to see what had been written on it.

"You chose the direction we went in," Ila murmured.

"Yes, because I have the light," snapped Alice, loudly, too loudly. The peace was disturbed.

"Just because you have the fucking torch doesn't mean... look, both these branches are identical, it doesn't even matter, right?"

They were pressed close to each other. Hannah felt, strangely, that her exclusion from the argument was intentional; neither asked for her opinion on where they should go next. There were doors all the way down this corridor, and Alice had tried to open each and every one as they passed them, but none of them opened. The argument kept going, slightly out of clear earshot, and Hannah looked down at the floorboards. The words on them were different from the graffiti on the walls. These seemed more articulate. *Sick so sick,* went one, older piece, carved deeply. *Sick so sick so sick.* Next to it, in much smaller, neater words, *they have forgotten have they not they forget what keeps them here safe from the outsiders. I will rise up again.* That one was written a lot, in lots of different hands, ones seeming newer and ones seeming far older. *I will rise up again in the new dawn,* one of them continued. *It will be a glad day.*

Her heart stopped when she saw what was chiseled into the wood next to that one. She stood up and stepped away from the words as if they were toxic to her. It had to be nothing, surely... some sick coincidence. Lots of people had the same name as her. It could be referring to anyone.

And yet. It said, *Hannah you are home.*

Even when she looked away from it, the words were there,

in her head. *Hannah you are home, Hannah you are home*. She didn't feel that she was home at all. She wanted to leave. There was something very, very wrong about this house, and she felt that if she didn't leave now, she would never leave at all.

"Alice," she said, "Ila, I want to go."

Their murmuring had ceased, and the argument had, she guessed, been resolved. But there was no answer to her. She looked to her left, and then to her right, and there was no light at all, no sign of the torch beam.

"Hey!" she shouted, as loud as she could. It was a deep sin, she was sure, to shout here, but she had to – they had probably just wandered off, forgetting about her, always leaving her behind, always forgetting about her because she was small and, she secretly thought, they didn't actually care, did they, they just liked having her there, they didn't want her to leave, that's why Alice hated her boyfriend, that's why they had left her now alone in the dark and why they weren't responding to her screaming for help at all.

"Help!" she shouted again.

The House gulped down her voice. It didn't echo. Wherever they had gone, they couldn't hear her. And like that, Hannah was lost. She turned to the direction she thought they had come from, the route that would lead her straight back to the first-floor landing. That would still be dark, but it would be somewhere she *knew* and maybe, just maybe, Hannah would be able to make her way down the stairs and out into the outside, which suddenly seemed like the safest place possible. She had to put her hand out to feel the wall, and it was good to know that it was there, something real. Her other hand gripped the right shoulder strap of her rucksack again. As she moved down the corridor, she felt the things carved into the wall running beneath her fingers. Her footsteps thumped beneath her. Every now and then, there would be a door. She couldn't see it, but she could feel it with her hand. She already knew none of them would open. There was no point in even trying. The best way to go was straight on.

At the end of this corridor, Hannah was sure there would be the landing. The walls and the ceiling of the corridor felt violent compared to the open space of the landing, which was about to come, any moment, the landing would be there, she would stumble out into it and the air would be less dry in her throat. But there was only darkness. The corridor stretched on and on, longer than it had been before. Longer than it could logically be. The patterns beneath her hand started to feel familiar. It came to her then, although she wasn't sure why or how it had landed in her head: this was the same stretch of corridor, over and over, looping like a Moebius strip. There was no end. There never would be.

She screamed, again, pointlessly. "Help!" She stood still and listened as the word was eaten up by the darkness. There was no presence around her, nothing behind or in front. Something wet was on her cheeks. She rubbed her eyes.

Stupid little girl, crying because she's lost, stupid little girl.

Those words... it wasn't clear if they were her own. They came to her like her own thoughts, but they had a voice which was not hers.

Every child gets lost, in the woods, in the supermarket. Hannah remembered this. She was six, and had been walking behind her mum, the bright lights and colours of capitalism reflecting in her eyes. And then, quite suddenly, her mum was gone. Little Hannah ran to a woman who she was sure looked like her, but the woman turned and it wasn't her mum at all, it was some other woman with straw coloured hair. Her face, to Hannah, looked like an old leather sofa. "Are you lost?" she asked.

Again, Hannah put her hand out to the wall, and was shocked to find that it was now *warm*. Warm and alive. Hannah lent in and pressed her ear to it. There was a movement, from deep within the House. Shifting in and out. Deep breaths.

Hannah started to run, but her feet were unsteady. She ran without certainty of which direction she was headed in, and knowing, of course, that it didn't matter one bit. It was dark as night behind her, but, suddenly, the way ahead seemed to be illuminated, if only very slightly. The walls, and the locked doors embedded in them, were visible to her. The wallpaper, peeling off in strips, the ceiling, cracked, the words and images on the floor and the wall. She could see them, slightly at first, but as she ran, nearly falling over her own feet, her heartbeat deafening in her head, they became clearer and clearer.

Hannah you are home.

She propelled herself as fast as she could, passing a violent, detailed carving of a woman with her eyes crossed out and her vagina being stretched open by some kind of medical instrument. Passing more words, bigger words, those same words, *Hannah you are home, Hannah you are home.* There were no more doors now, just walls, stretching out in front of her. There was only ahead, which was light, which was progress, and behind, which was dark, hallowed, cold. And that light which pulled her in was all red.

Then came the door. Up ahead. She stopped running, and nearly tumbled onto the floorboard with shock at its sudden existence. A door, in the distance, but definitely real, and not off to the side like the others had been. This one was a dead end to the corridor. It was open. Ajar. There was more of that same light, blazing through the crack, bright and red and glorious and living. It made her feel special. She let her bag slip from her shoulder onto the ground and left it there. As she walked now, with the words looping in spirals around the walls and floor and ceiling, the words repeating their welcome, their affirmation, *Hannah you are home, Hannah you are home, Hannah you are home, Hannah you are home, Hannah you are home,* twisting around her like comforting arms. The door opened fully, and she walked into the threshold of the room. The walls were bright with the red. They were entirely unblemished. Looking at them hurt, but she looked at them anyway. She felt safe, like she had crawled back inside the womb. The House had no electricity, but the lightbulb burned from the ceiling anyway. The room throbbed. The walls weren't solid. The red settled on her, bathing her. The words were not written around the walls here, but they rattled in her head anyway, and they rang true. Yes, she was, Hannah was home.

ALICE AND/OR ILA

Hannah had been there one moment, and then, when they turned back, after deciding on a direction to go, she was gone.

Ila swore.

Alice pointed the torch down the other branch of the corridor, but there was no sign of her. She turned and pointed it back the way they came, but still, no Hannah. If she had walked off somewhere, it was beyond the reach of the torchlight. Ila was still standing behind her, the constant stream of "fuck, fuck, fuck," weirdly reassuring. Ila, at least, was there, and as long as Alice could hear her, she knew that.

"Hannah!" shouted Alice. There was no answer.

"We have to turn back," said Ila. "She could be back on the landing."

"She could just as easily have gone down the other branch. And if we go back to the landing, we'll be leaving her there, getting further away from her."

"Well, shit," said Ila. She pushed Alice as hard as she could. "Fuck you! This is your fault!"

"How? She wandered off!"

"No!" Ila's eyes were wild, brimming with tears. "No, no, this was your stupid, virtue signalling idea, that coming here could mean something, that this would represent something, because you couldn't admit that you just thought it would be funny to do some breaking and entering. And now Hannah isn't here."

"No, she isn't," agreed Alice, doing her best to keep her voice calm. "And every second we stand still she stays lost."

"So where do we go?"

Alice thought. "If she went back to the landing, then she's out of this maze of corridors, right? But if she went deeper in, then... we should go deeper."

Neither of them wanted to talk about the obvious thing, which was that Hannah wasn't calling for them, or responding to their calls. But they turned. They had been standing in the way of one of the two branches, so there was only one she could have gone down, if she hadn't headed back. And they started to walk. Ila put her hand out and grasped Alice's fingers tightly, despite how angry she was at her. They followed the corridor, looking at the circle of light. Every now and then they called for Hannah. Sometimes, Alice would stop, silently, and try one of the doors they passed, but they were, of course, all locked, or rusted shut. They kept going, kept calling, following the corridor as long as they could, passing countless slurs cut into the walls on either side of them.

"Hannah!" shouted Ila.

No answer.

At first, they thought the light had found a dead end, and their stomachs dropped. But then Ila realised it was actually a corner. It got closer. On the wall ahead, somebody, somewhen, had written *fucking bitches* with a blade.

They turned the corner and there it was. The corridor stretched ahead, and ended, abruptly, with the door. Alice's torch showed it clearly. It was ajar, and inside was darkness. They walked faster, hands still joined, their footsteps the only things in the world, the door rushing towards them. They didn't stop to see what was written on the walls around them, if anything was written on them at all. Alice pushed the door open, terrified about what she would find in there.

It was dark, and she moved the torchlight across the room. She saw the desk, pushed against the wall. The door, the second door, shut tightly on the other side of the room. Hannah was standing opposite with her back to them, pressing her face into the wallpaper. Her arms outstretched, palms turned inwards.

"Hannah," breathed Ila.

Hannah turned towards them. She was pale in the beam of the torchlight. As pale as a ghost.

"Hello Ila," she said, in a quiet voice. "Are you okay?"

"What happened?"

Ila wanted to go to her and embrace the girl, but she didn't. There was something wrong. Hannah crackled like static. She looked up at the ceiling. Her face was blank, yet Alice couldn't help but project emotion onto it, reading hurt into Hannah's motionless mouth and her wide eyes. Those eyes searched for something on the expanse of the ceiling before settling on the single anachronistic bulb which hung from its wire lifelessly. She stared at it, blinked, and the lightbulb was illuminated. Alice dropped the torch onto the floor. Her eyes had grown used to the gloom and the torch-light, so now, with the room properly lit, it felt like she was staring into the heart of an explosion. She had to screw her eyes shut from the pain before she could slowly open them again, and it was still too much, really, it still hurt her eyes. Ila had to put her hands up over her face until she was used to the jarring brightness. The torch rolled a little as it hit the floor, and then stayed still, its beam still on but utterly useless now. Hannah hadn't even blinked.

The room seemed to come alive around them. The red of the walls intruded in on the space, dribbling and pooling beneath their feet, washing everything clean. The walls themselves may have been pressing in to crush them, or they may have been far off, barely visible in the distance, or they may have been both at once. And the ceiling, was that pressing down from above, or was it as tall and wide as the open sky?

By all rights Hannah had been staring straight at the unshaded lightbulb long enough to have caused herself some serious damage, but she didn't seem to mind. She just looked up. Her mouth twisted upwards in a half smile. Then her retinas flicked down and she beheld the two of them. There were tears beginning to well up and wet her cheeks. She looked at them, and Alice could have sworn her eyes, which had once been blue, were being diluted with the room's colour. Going red, gradually, and growing brighter too.

"You've never treated me well, have you?"

The voice that floated from between her lips was high and girlish, like the one she affected to get free drinks at a bar. Her hair was more golden than it had ever been before. It glimmered as a halo around her. She appeared as some pre-Raphaelite painting, some kind of perfect, flawless muse, with skin as white as the canvas it was painted on.

"What?"

Ila moved backwards. Alice stood behind and closed her arms around her in a protective embrace.

"Neither of you ever treated me well."

Hannah lifted her arms forwards, palms facing upwards. *Here I am, the embodiment of grace.*

"I never knew why. I always thought, ridiculously, that I just wasn't cool enough for either of you. I bought into it. You were so much better than me in every way. So much cleverer. So much more interesting. But now, I know. Now I'm home, I know."

"Home?" asked Alice. She gripped Ila tightly.

"You hated me because I was better than you."

"What?"

Hannah's voice had previously been calm, and her face had been blank. But now pain started to intrude into her speech. Pain, anger, and hate. Her eyes glimmered brighter. Her mouth twisted, as if every syllable was coated with razor blades.

"Because... because I'm just better. Look at me. Look at you."

She screwed her palms shut into fists. Tremors rippled through her body like she was having some kind of fit.

"You two, fucking on the beach after that fucking parade. You thought I didn't see, you thought I was asleep, but I saw and it made me sick. You fill me with bile, you disgust me, you hated me because I was too perfect for you, too pale, too blonde, it told me all about it, it told me and I knew it was true, fucking dykes, fucking fags, fucking pa-" the words spilled out of her like sickness.

She doubled over then, bending in on herself as something sharp jabbed at her guts. "Fucking." It was difficult for her to speak. Every dark instinct within squeezed through her body and out of her mouth. Every terrible thing in the world. Her head bent upwards unnaturally, looking up again. The light reflected in her eyes. Yes. They were red now. Red, and hot as a sun. There was spit foaming around her lips, bubbling down her chin unbidden.

"As I look ahead, I am filled with foreboding; like the Roman, I seem to see the River Tiber foaming with much blood. And as I look ahead I see this, that I loved you but now I see. I loved you but now I'm home and I have always been home and I will always be home. And this home is not made for you."

She swayed, and was struck by some great, unseen force that made her stumble backwards, yelping in pain. She nearly fell, until her body was leaning against the far wall, and her arms were splayed out on either side of her, rigid.

"It's okay," Ila said, trying to keep her voice free of the immeasurable rising panic that was within her. "You're just hurt." She wanted to embrace Hannah. *She doesn't know what she's saying*, she told herself. "You're having some kind of... we'll call an ambulance or something."

"You can't just call an ambulance on someone," said Alice, quietly but sharply into her ear. "They won't just send paramedics, they'll probably bring the police as well!"

"Well what else do we do? We can't take her to hospital, can we? We probably can't even safely move her from this room." Ila snarled. "Look at her. She's not right."

"She just called you..."

Hannah arched back and her arms, which had been so straight, suddenly contorted, twisting around behind her, fingers grabbing uselessly at nothing. From within her came a scream of horror. She screamed, and her body spasmed, stuck in an unnatural position, her arms knotting behind her back.

"Tranny!" she shouted, with all the force in her lungs. "Fucking tranny! Fucking tyranny!"

The words were wet, every syllable came with a further bubbling of fluid. Ila thought she might bite off her own tongue.

All Ila could say was "She's ill. She's having some kind of psychotic break."

Behind the two of them, the door to the room swung shut on its own. Ila ran to it and tried to force it back open, but the door felt as if it had not only been locked but welded, merged to become part of the door. There was no exit.

"Help me, Alice," she shouted, but even with both of their full weight pushing the door didn't shift. Even as they tried to open the door, a noise came from behind them. They turned to look at Hannah. She was still leaning against the wall. Her mouth was open, but no words or screams left her now. Her mouth opened and shut, like she was trying to speak still, but found it impossible. The only sound she produced was a gurgling, her breathing ragged. Just a few moments ago, Hannah had appeared as a saint, or an angel, but now her hair was tangled over her face, and the white of her skin looked more like the symptom of a sickness than anything else. Her arms were still tangled around together, and Alice and Ila heard a cracking as the bones within them gave into the strain. Then her right arm suddenly shot out and up. There was more crunching. The arm was held at a strange angle to the rest of her, an angle that would never have been possible for Hannah to make on her own. Something was using her, bending her, without care. As the bone shattered, the skin seemed to stay unbroken, although they could see it rippling. Her eyes were still looking upwards. Staring heavensward. Her right leg was pulled out from under her by something unseen, but she stayed upright still. It was manipulated, bent to the side at another sharp angle. Her other arm was pulled up, too. Hannah's hands were still grasping at air, sometimes managing to touch the wall where she dug her nails in, only to have her hands pulled away by force. *No, not like that like this.* A great force puzzled through her body, twisting her towards its own ends. Each limb pulled until it stayed in a right angle to the body, and with every movement there came a chorus of splintering bones. Her arms and legs bent again, and then her body was pulled to the side, and there she was. The House had turned her into a swastika. It had used her body as a material to mould it, and now it held her up, showing her off to them like a proud little boy who had just drawn his first crayon picture. *Look at this. Look at what I made. Don't you think it is pretty, don't you think she's pretty?*

"The day will come," Hannah said, quieter now, in a voice that was very far from hers. "The glad day will come and he will rise and this country will be cleansed by his waves. He was the first man in this land, and he will be the last."

Liquid dripped from her mouth and down the front of her clothes. Her eyes looked down at them again. The redness had spilled through them, breaking the retinas, breaking the blood vessels. And yet, Alice was sure those eyes still saw them. The room was small but it suddenly felt like an impassable space. A whole country stretched between them and Hannah. A whole continent swirling with red. Piss soaked Hannah's skirt, and she lost control of her bowels, too. She spoke again, this time in her own voice.

"It said I would be safe."

The words came from far away, but she felt every moment of it. It would be a great betrayal.

Both Ila and Alice sobbed. The light blazed down, illuminating Hannah's shattered body. Ila's gut twisted inside her at the sight of the thing. Alice let her go, after holding her painfully hard during the mutilation, and now, free of her grasp, she stumbled a little away from Alice to throw up onto the wooden floor. The sick splattered. Alice looked away from it. Ila threw up what she thought was everything she had, but her legs were shaking, unstable. When she tried to walk back to Alice, her legs gave up completely, and Ila fell face first into her own sick. She tried to lift herself up, but her hands slipped on it and she fell back down into the sick again. So she just lay there. Beneath the reflecting red of the wall. The white from above settling on her body. She cried, harder and deeper than she ever had. Alice tried to kick open the door, but it wouldn't move, however hard she kicked. It felt like there was nothing on the other side of the door – that it wasn't a door at all, but the border to the world, and the inside of this room was the entire world. If you were to open the door you would find… what?

The world outside is dark and unknowable. In the room you are safe. You are subject to violence, abuse, mistreatment, hurt, pain, all of the above, but you are safe from what is outside the room and that is what matters, inside the room is the pain you know, outside the room is the pain you do not know, it's not a hard choice to make in the end, to sit here 'neath the burning sun of her body, her body once a symbol of peace and now look at it look at what they did to her look at how much pain she is in look see, she's begging you, my heart beats around you, my stomach begins to dissolve you, yet I have no organs yet I have a body yet I have no head yet I am a body so far beneath the earth that nobody would ever think to find my bones here I am, reaching out to you, here you are, standing on top of me, they built a new world on me, they will build a new world on me…

Hannah saw what happened next. One instance with one eye, and one with the other. The room split in two as she looked on, helpless and trembling.

In one eye, Hannah saw this: Ila lay in the puddle of her own sick, heaving great sobs deep through her body. She had no way of comprehending what had happened to her friend, and had shut down in response, let herself go prone and helpless. Which made it easier, really. Alice was still standing at the door, looking from Ila to Hannah and back again. Her stare had grown strangely blank, like she had left this place and fallen to somewhere else. Then she walked, like a dreamer, across the room. Hannah watched with one eye, while the other was elsewhere. It was not a clean split. Both visions bled into the other. The border that

In one eye, Hannah saw this: Whilst Ila lay there in the puddle of her vomit, Alice sat down close to her, anxious about her friend.

"Ila?" She reached out a hand to stroke her hair, but Ila didn't respond at all. *None of this is happening,* Alice repeated to herself with every heartbeat. But the room felt real around her, and Hannah's living corpse looked real, and Ila was there, she could feel her. She stroked her hair. It was a mess. Little balls of sick stuck to the strands.

They sat like this for eternity. They sat like this even as Hannah's other eye saw Alice with the scalpel, and saw what she was going to do. Hannah held lay between realities was a jagged wound. Alice walked across the room, like a dreamer. She walked with purpose to the desk pushed against the wall. Her hands opened it and felt around for something inside which she knew would be there. A scalpel. Small and bright. It had been in the room for as long as the room existed, yet it was as sharp as if it had been made only yesterday. Ila didn't notice any of these. She just lay there. Sobbing in her own vomit. Alice returned, moving carefully to her friend. She bent over Ila and brushed the hair from her face.

"Come on," she whispered, care in her words. "Let's get you up."

Ila let herself be pulled up by Alice, her face dripping wet. She put her arms around Alice's on to this other, peaceful vision with everything she had. Alice would not hurt Ila. She couldn't. And that was what she was telling herself, as Ila sprung, suddenly, from her vegetative state, and smashed the back of her right hand into Alice's face, knocking her to the floor. Alice scrambled, trying to pull herself back up, but Ila stood up, as if she had never fallen, and kicked Alice over and over in the stomach. The first kick knocked all of the fight out of her. The second knocked the rest of her breath out. She was helpless, but Ila kicked until she could see bright stars on the ceiling above.

Alice's torch was still there, by the door. Forgotten in the brightness of the room. Ila reached shoulders and sobbed into her chest. Alice placed one hand on the top of her head and, out of nowhere, slammed Ila back down onto the floor, face first into the sick again. Ila screamed, starting to struggle, but Alice had her completely: she lifted her up again, now with no tenderness at all, and smashed her face into the floorboard a second time. When Ila rolled over to look up at her, there was blood pouring from her nose and mouth.

"What are you doing?" she spluttered.

"Taking care of you," said Alice, wiping blood and snot away from her cheek. "Stay still now, okay?"

Ila didn't want to stay still. But Alice held that scalpel up in front of her face and nodded. See. This is why you have to do for it. Alice didn't want to look. She shut her eyes and hoped that this truly wasn't real, but it felt real. Those kicks had felt real. It felt real when Ila lifted her skirt up and pulled her underwear to the side.

"Please," murmured Alice.

"Please what?"

"Please don't."

Ila seemed to think about this. Her eyes were red with blood and earth. She lifted up one of Alice's legs, exposing her hormone-shrunken dick, hairless and pink, and there, the eye of her asshole. Ila used the other hand to jam the torch, hard, into it, pushing as far up into Alice's guts as she could get, stretching it out. Blood and shit dribbled out. Alice screamed, finding an energy which what I tell you. This is why you have to let me do it. Alice cut down the length of Ila's clothes, exposing her stomach and then her crotch, too. She hooked the scalpel gently inside Ila's underwear and tore them off her body. Her hand, with the blade in it, hovered over Ila's stomach.

The cuts weren't deep. But they were deep enough. Blood seeped down in thin lines, dripping, bright with the freshness of the cuts. The words weren't deep, but they were deep enough to scar, and in a year's time Ila will still have them on her, still feel horror and shame whenever she sees them. In one year, in three years. Forever.

Alice pulled apart Ila's legs, the scalpel still glimmering in one hand. Hannah, floating helplessly,

hadn't been there before. She screamed, but her body was too weak to fight back. The torch was still on. One unblinking eye, shining up at Ila. Searing into her vision. Ila pulled the torch back out halfway, and the pain subsided for a second before she pushed it in again. Hannah wanted to scream and cry and embrace her friends close. She cursed the room, cursed the thoughts it had given her, cursed the words the House had put into her mouth, even as she knew they were as much her words as they were Albion's. The House had simply let them free. Alice passed from consciousness, and when she came back to the world, the torch had been removed from her insides, and Ila was holding the scalpel. Alice didn't wanted to scream out, to try and stop what was happening. She could see the room settling within Alice, as she could see it settling within Ila, too, from her other eye. But it had her, and that was it. She could only hang there like a desiccated Christ on a desiccated cross and watch as Alice pushed her dick up inside of Ila, and by this point Ila couldn't say anything at all. Alice didn't cum. She only managed a few thrusts inside before she started to go soft. She was on antidepressants and hormones that made orgasm practically impossible anyway. When she went soft, she pulled out and stood up. Her skirt fell back into place. She stepped away from Ila, who was sprawled and utterly motionless. She stepped

recognise it. Hannah did. Hannah knew the scalpel well, from her other eye. Ila brushed the hair from Alice's face and there, in the dead centre of her blemishless forehead, she carved the smooth diamond of a cunt.

"You will always know," she said, "what you aren't." And she left, without the scalpel or the torch. It took a long while for Alice to pull herself up, and when she did she was barely able to walk. Her insides felt like they'd been pulped. The House let her leave the room. It threw her out onto the street, and the cold air stung the cunt on her head. Somebody across the road was walking their dog, and they called an ambulance, and she asked them to take her home.

away towards the door. It opened. Outside was the world, as it had always been. As she left the room, Alice dropped the scalpel under her feet. When she had gone, Ila pulled herself up, wincing with the pain of movement. She grabbed hold of the scalpel and brought it back to her. Her thigh was exposed, and, without even looking, she cut a word that girls at school used to call her into her leg, a word which looked sometimes like *panic* but was not. She waited to die beneath Hannah's gaze, but she didn't. When it became clear that she wasn't going to, she pulled herself up and stumbled from the room. Behind her, the door slammed shut, and Hannah was alone.

Hannah saw them leave. The two split instances melded together once they were gone. She hung there for quite some time, not alive, not dead. Her body began to rot. The flesh fell away, exposing the bones beneath. The longer she stayed a swastika, it seemed that she had always, deep down, been a swastika. This was just her true self. It had finally been achieved, expressed in euphoric ecstasy, glimmering with fresh dew. She hung there. At first a girl, then a symbol, then a stain on the wall. The House swallowed her, and inside it she found that she wasn't alone. There were hundreds of girls buried within. Girls without eyes, girls without heads, girls without wombs. Giant holes cut into their bodies to pull things out, unravelled and pleading for help that would never come. Martyred girls, mutilated girls, girls that Hannah thought, in her darkest moments, deserved what they had gotten. They all huddled close to one another for warmth.

"A glad day will come," one of them said, but Hannah had no idea if she believed the words. We are all here now. We wait for you. Irreversibly damaged.

"The weeping child could not be heard,
The weeping parents wept in vain:
They stripped him to his little shirt,
And bound him in an iron chain,

And burned him in a holy place
Where many had been burned before;
The weeping parents wept in vain.
Are such things done on Albion's shore?"

William Blake, "A Little Boy Lost"

PART 3

THE DANCE OF ALBION

HOUSE

Alice or Ila stumbled out into the light of day. Three girls had gone into the house believing in something, and now only two had left, believing in something else entirely. Or at least, that was how it seemed. It had always been there, hadn't it? The potential within them. It just took the House to show them that.

Neither of them were ever questioned by the police. The police were, of course, linked to the House by a thin but unbreakable thread. Alice felt almost jealous of those who *were* questioned – they were Hannah's closest friends, after all... but she was glad that she didn't have to try and pretend that she knew nothing. Ila told nobody the full extent of it. She attempted suicide more than once, she went on and off her medications. Alice drank an obscene amount, took drugs until she felt like she wasn't even there. She grew a second layer of harder skin, as a protective measure. It was around this time that Alice began to see the ghosts. At first, she wasn't sure if they were hallucinations. But she decided that these ghosts must be connected to the House, and so she learned to live with them.

There were multiple suspects in Hannah's disappearance, the primary one being Brandon, who had been her boyfriend when she vanished. Police found evidence that he had been seen outside of Hannah's property on more than one occasion since her disappearance. He said he was grieving and confused. Sometimes he walked there, to her flat, fully believing she was waiting for him, only to remember. He claimed that there was no real evidence against him, and the police were enacting a racial bias against a young black man, assuming that he was responsible. He tried to tell the authorities to question Alice and Ila, but they seemed uninterested. He was never formally charged.

Hannah's parents recorded three television messages and one radio message, pleading for her to come home, or at least contact somebody if she was able to.

Over time, Hannah's suspended form began to sink into the wall behind her, leaving the perfect, vivid red paper irreparably stained.

The House stayed where it was. The room kept beating inside of it, the bloody heart of England staying still and strong until its new era dawned. It knew that the time would come soon. With every year, it ate more and more tabloid headlines, gorging itself sick on them. They tried to tear it apart. They tried to turn it into flats. It didn't let them. Not yet, in any case.

ILA

They lay in Ila's bed looking at the ceiling for half an hour after fucking, trying to clear their heads of the violent intrusive thoughts that had resurfaced, unbidden. The ceiling of Ila's flat used to be riddled with cracks. Alice remembered how in the past they would trace them together, wondering if the whole building was about to collapse in on them.

Ila pulls herself out of the stupor. She is meant to pee, she always forgets that she is meant to pee after sex. She vanishes off to the bathroom. When she returns, she stands in the doorway, still naked. The two girls look at each other, saying nothing, both thinking the same thing: this was a mistake. Neither of them had orgasmed. Neither of them had even really enjoyed themselves. It just felt like they were *supposed* to fuck. It felt natural, but it was not something that either of them had really wanted. Alice had held out some vague hope that the years of hate between them might add an element of raw sexual energy to it, but it didn't. It felt like an apathetic repetition of something they used to do back in days where things didn't seem so complicated.

"Did you do this one?" asks Ila, pointing at the unreadable word on her leg, the word she thought might be *panic* but wasn't.

Alice shrugs. "I didn't do any of them."

"Sure."

Ila lay back down next to her. There was that unspoken gulf between them. They both remembered what had happened so differently. Memory is a difficult thing to navigate, especially traumatic memory. It splinters. You can cut yourself on the edges of it so easily.

Ila's room seemed to be just as haunted as Alice's own, but Ila claimed that she had never witnessed anything in here that was not directly something she could touch or explain. Out of the window, there was an abandoned office block visible. When one of the companies stationed there had folded, five of its employees had taken the lift up to the roof and tried to jump. None of them had done it. But the intent had been there. The urge to jump and let the ground rush up to you. This had been a long time before Ila lived there though. The old woman who lived upstairs had told her about it, she was a Romanian immigrant. Like Alice, she burned incense to smoke out the evil things, and they could even smell it down here lying on Ila's bed. It smells heavy, like sleep, and covers up the funk of sex somewhat.

While Alice had been inside of Ila, Ila, on top, had wondered if she could choke Alice to death. She was choking her anyway, sexually, trying to kindle something. It hadn't worked at all. But the compulsion had been there. It would have been so easy... but the red voice said no, don't. Bring her back to the House and let it happen there. Let it tie itself up neatly in a bow. When riding the girl's cock, every time Ila saw Alice's face, she saw the cunt on her forehead dripping with sweat. It had seemed to be gaping open wide.

Now they were done. Back on the bed, Ila drinks from an open can of beer, which has just started to flatten. "Thanks," she says. "For the sex, I mean."

"When was the last time you fucked someone?" Alice pulls herself up to a sitting position.

Ila shrugs. "I think it was the one I got cancelled for."

"Joyce?"

"No, no, I never fucked her. She came onto me in the bathroom, the old creep. Nearly did it, too. She's just bitter now that she didn't get to. I mean the other one, the one who said I called her..."

"A tranny?"

"Mhmm." There is a silence. "What about you? When was the last time you got some?"

"I brought someone home from a party, but she got scared off by a ghost."

Ila is not sure if she's being serious or not, but then again, she never has been, even back when they were friends, Alice would say things which seemed like jokes, but there was truth to them.

There is nothing left of the singer now, wherever he is.

"You know," says Ila, looking at the beer in her hand, "whatever happened, I missed you."

Alice tries to catch her eyes. "You went on Radio Four and said that the government should ban people like me from being in public."

"I did *not*, I was making an argument about the importance of spaces for women—"

"And I'm not a woman?" Alice asked. The sad tenderness which had seeped into the room was now gone. Everything was sharp.

"I didn't say that, did I, you fucking idiot. This is your problem, Alice,—" she tries to finish her beer but realises that there's basically none left, so she crumples the can and throws it against the wall "—you just decide to automatically read what people say as the worst possible outcome, you take public safety as a personal attack on you! It isn't about you! No one cares what you think!"

"No one cares what you think either." Alice gets out of the bed. "You're a fucking sell out, and you know they only care about you because you make them look less white. Half of their shit is antisemitic conspiracies, and you're a Jew happily peddling them." Alice tries to put on her shirt, but she puts it on backwards, so she has to take it off again to put it on properly.

"Since when did you care about antisemitism?" Ila snarls.

Alice doesn't answer.

"Don't you fucking ignore me. You can't walk out of this, remember, we're going to the House, we're going to exorcise this, I'm sure you'll want to be there so you can rape me half to death again in front of our friend's corpse…"

She grabs Alice's hand hard, and Alice tries to tear herself away but finds herself being pulled back onto the bed. They look into each other's eyes.

"Fuck you," says Alice.

"Fuck you," says Ila.

And they fuck again. This time, it isn't quite so boring. Alice lets Ila fuck her in the ass with the strap-on, and she feels something like peace. When Ila is inside her, Alice, with her legs up in the air, looks into her friend's eyes.

"Call me it, please," she says.

"Call you what?"

"You know. You know you want to, as well."

She hesitates for a moment. But Alice is right. She does want to.

"You fucking tranny," Ila moans.

"God. Fuck. Please." The pleasure is nearly unbearable for Alice. "Do it again. Tell me what you think of me, what you really think of me. Tell me I'm nothing. Tell me I'm worthless."

"You," Ila grabs Alice's hair, "are a fucking worthless tranny."

"Yes."

"You are a fucking plague on this country. You convert helpless young girls into your sick cult. You make them mutilate their bodies, bind and cut off their breasts, until they are so gaslit into the trans ideology that they think they are happy. You are just a man, and even if you had a cunt between your legs, it wouldn't be real, it would just be an open wound that your body rejects." She slaps Alice in the face whilst fucking her. It leaves a scarlet mark on her cheek. "You're a threat to women. Everybody sees you and thinks you're disgusting. Everybody sees you and thinks, who the fuck is that man in a dress and makeup, trying to hide his bulge. Who the fuck does he think he is? Your dick's too big to hide. Your bulge when you wear a skirt looks so gross."

"Yes!" Alice is writhing beneath her.

"You aren't a woman, you're a deviant, you aren't a fucking woman!"

"What are you going to do to me?"

Ila leans down close and spits the words out. "I'm going to eradicate you."

Alice screams, "yes", she screams yes and she cums properly for the first time in months. She imagines that there is a pair of eyes frozen in space watching her cum, watching from within the walls of Ila's flat.

And then they are lying in each other's grasp drifting in and out of consciousness. For a moment the world reverts to an alternative, where events took a different course; where they loved each other and felt less ashamed of each other's difference, because even before she posted about it online, Ila was uncomfortable with Alice, they were best friends, they fucked once a week when drunk or high, but she felt sick afterwards when she thought about her body and what their bodies had done together, and Alice couldn't forget Ila's immigrant family and wondered if they had taken British workers' jobs, even though she knew that was a horrible thing to think about, she thought that there was maybe actually possibly a left-wing case for border control when you looked at it, not that she really agreed but likc – the implications of mass immigration to the UK – I mean, the average white worker too was anti-immigration, surely you had to think of him, surely you had to listen to what he thought, his thoughts were as valid as anyone else's right? And, she thought, she thinks, if you looked at it, the billionaire class actually wants immigration, they want it, they want wide movements of workers, and obviously this is a disgusting way to think but it is how she thinks, she's nothing if not honest, and, and... Ila always hated going into public bathrooms with Alice, even though they'd fucked many times, it was more that she thought other women would see her with Alice and think that she, Ila, also had a dick, and judge her for that.

What is a woman? That's always the question, isn't it? What was a woman, and what now is a woman, in the new world, can a woman be nothing more than a handful of flesh and skin shaped into offensive images, and, well, people say look at the Nazi's, they burned the books on trans people, and she feels sick when they say that because her grandma actually fled the Holocaust and what did she get from that? A nose she hates and people not believing that she can be two things at once, and people thinking that she must have strong opinions on Israel either way because she's either brown or Jewish but not both, but she feels sick when people say Hitler killed trans people, even if it's technically true it feels like they are removing her own arteries and wrapping them around her throat and choking her with them. And Alice did once listen to a podcast where they said, well now we aren't antisemitic, but it's strange all this billionaire rapists are Jewish, and it had been meant as a joke probably but she'd never been able to tell, and who runs the factory, the factory that is a tower with the spectre behind her, whatever that presence had been, Ila or Hannah or her own mother or herself, who *owned* the tower, hey, that's all she's saying, that's all she's asking, follow the money, anonymously of course, she doesn't want to have people coming for her, and would Ila have people coming for her in real life, now they thought she was a sex creep who liked to say slurs during sex (now they knew she was a sex creep who liked to say slurs during sex)? Just another Jewish sex creep, thinks Alice, and decides she only meant that as a joke. She decides this only after she has already thought it.

Are you a bad person, or do you just have reasonable concerns, are you a bad person, or are you just asking questions? In the crushed heat death you ask how to win a culture war, and when does a culture war become a real war, where is the line that is crossed, is it the spilling of blood and has blood already spilled? It must be a war to be called a war. If you call something something, it becomes something, if you call a tower a factory, then it's a factory, and we have to take you for your word, take it as it comes, take it on the chin, keep calm and carry on in Churchill's Britain with his statue all covered in protective wood to stop the masses from clawing at it. And what right does anyone have to think on any of this, let alone try and put it into words, especially a white woman, white women are symbols, white women as symbols, white woman are *literally* symbols and whether that's somehow still too subtle, and why write when you feel guilty, where were you when we lost the culture war? This is how you lost the culture war: you were kneeling in front of a swastika made of white flesh, you were in a forest somewhere, a group of boys suspending a plank with a rusted nail over your young soft brain, you were getting raped in your girlfriend's bed whilst Come on Eileen by Dexys Midnight Runners played from her phone, you were meeting and drinking in a pub laughing with those names you aren't allowed to print for fear of legal action – so much for free speech – but they are the new wave of British intellectual, dark web fascism creeping into, out of, through, and around the borders of the British academy. You talked to a Trotskyist and he told you that he thought the London riots were a bad thing, that they had no revolutionary potential at all. You nearly spat in his drink. You couldn't believe he said it, although every person out of the sphere of leftism probably agrees with him. And then raining from the sky you see it all clear and lucid: free speech, de-platforming, suing students for calling you a TERF, getting an OBE but still being silenced, getting a book deal but still being silenced, wearing a mask which says CENSORED but still being silenced, being the establishment and the anti-establishment too, all at once, the King and the revolutionary as well, the whole discourse cycle one long endless ouroboros sucking on its own clit, it makes you scream, the state of the world and the state of the Union, it makes you scream because you know that truly you can't change a single thing in this godforsaken country, a country so racist that it will vote to kill its own immune system right before a global pandemic, a country so racist that the very ground stinks, a country so racist that your seemingly left-liberal parents have a map of the British Empire hanging on their wall and don't really question it at all, which, I suppose, means they aren't left-liberal at all, doesn't it, and your mum has a show called *Trans Kids: We Need to Talk* recorded onto the TV box but she's never watched it, where every time travellers move into an area they find themselves in danger because I guess racism doesn't count when it's towards them for most people, because bigotry and hatred towards travellers is such an ingrained part of British culture that it is difficult to imagine a world where that isn't the case, a country so racist that it might as well all be a red room in a eugenics paedophile house in an undisclosed location which is in Brighton or Portsmouth or London or somewhere else entirely. Where were you when we lost the war?

In a House. That's where you were.

In a House where no live organism can continue to exist, you continue to exist. And now there you are again. And you will go back there as many times as you can until it fucking tears your guts out and leaves you truly, actually, dead and rotting, and then you'll have to stay there, in its walls, pressed close to all those other women it martyred for the common cause of reproducing fascism over and over and spreading it as rain across this nightmarish island we call Britain. I don't know what I believe, I just know I want to be free of it, truly. I just want to pull it out from under me, look at it beating in my hand and then crush it. This is what you should want, too. Try to make the best of a bad situation. British spirit, or something like that. Stiff upper lip.

ALICE

When I was about fifteen, I used the website Tumblr. It still exists, as far as I know. It was a strange place, and it's hard to even describe how the culture of it felt when you were part of it: at times welcoming and at times unbearably tense. It was the first time I really read about what being trans was, and it was also where I was sent endless anonymous messages telling me to kill myself. People would often accuse others of things, baselessly, and those accusations would stick to them however much they tried to shake them away. One of my Tumblr mutuals was accused of being a paedophile and a Nazi. We hadn't really talked much at all – she'd re-blogged my selfies a few times, and I hadn't thought much about that until people started to accuse her. I began to wonder what her intentions had been when she shared a fifteen-year-old's selfies. She denied these accusations, of course. Anyone would. She claimed that the people accusing her of being a paedophile and a Nazi were TERFS – and the problem was that some of them were. Or had, at least, started to share

TERF rhetoric onto their blogs. Which made sense... they had just been exploited by an older trans woman, and suddenly these other older women were telling them, oh, come join us. There's a pattern to this, and we don't have to accept it as normal. I didn't understand it at the time, I was just angry, angry and confused, but I get it now, with Ila spooning me. I understand why she is the way she is. I hope she understands why I am like I am, too.

"Are you sure you want to come with me?" Ila asks, sleepily.

"Why not?"

"Because..." I can't tell what is going on beneath her words. Is she having second thoughts? "...it could be dangerous."

"I thought you said it was just a building."

"It is."

"So..." I sit up and gaze down at her from above.

"Well, it could, I don't know. Be dangerous. They tried to convert it into flats. You know that, right? Since we were there."

I light another fag inside her room. It's filled with smoke, even with one of the windows open, filled enough that the lamp is shrouded with it.

"Have you seen it?"

"Not up close. I've looked from far off, but I couldn't see anything, not really. It was too dark."

The cigarette is good. I needed it. The reality of what going back means has started to dawn, now we've fucked and sealed our bond. She might say that it's 'just a building', but she knows she's lying, and I know she's lying, and we're still going back anyway.

I stopped using Tumblr shortly after that whole affair, and after having other people creep on me too – most notably a nineteen-year-old fat rights activist who seemed obsessed with my hair. I turned to 4chan and other forums in that vein, where, even if there were Nazis and paedophiles, at least they were generally honest about being those things, even as they remained anonymous. It felt better to know that I was talking to someone who liked to masturbate over little boys than to talk to someone and find that out about them later.

After I agreed to come back to Ila's flat, we got beer and got drunk and high and started to fuck. I never said, yes, I'll go back to the House with you. But in our union it was decided.

The worst thing is that I want to. I want to see the House now. I want to see if what happened was real.

I miss it.

That's the worst thing, actually. I miss it. I miss how it felt in that room. And you can't know how it felt unless you were there, in that pulsing red soul. I don't remember hurting Ila at all. But I remember feeling something, deep within, a power rising up my esophagus and crawling from my mouth. Did she feel like that when she shoved that torch inside of me? I thought I forgave you, Ila my love, but I'm not so sure. Now kiss me hard on the mouth.

"Didn't this building used to suck?"

Ila is slowly getting dressed, in the same clothes she was wearing before. We both smell of sweat, but it doesn't matter, really.

"Yeah."

She pulls her shirt over her head.

"The landlord did it up, and put up the rent as well. The Sudanese family next door couldn't afford it, and they spat on my door as they left. I was like, christ, why is this my fault? I mean, I didn't say that, but that's what I was thinking when I scrubbed the door clean."

"Evil landlord shit, though."

"Yeah." She rubs her nose. "Evil landlord shit."

That poor family, kicked out so that Ila could have a working lift. And then, at the same time, a horrible little voice asking what their immigration status was. Is that the House's voice? Or mine?

We get the lift down, and out of her building. It's freezing cold outside, and Ila, without thinking, takes my hand. I turn to her.

"Sorry," she says, and lets go.

"No, it's okay." I take her hand again. She feels chilly already.

"I just wasn't thinking, Alice."

"We can hold hands. If you want. I don't mind, I promise."

But maybe she just doesn't want to be seen hand-in-hand with a tranny. It's ten o'clock now, the streetlights are on. We leap from pool of light to pool of light. We only feel safe beneath them, where we can see our feet and each other's eyes clearly. So we keep going, ushering each other forwards. I wish I had coke with me. A homeless man asks me for money, but I shrug and say, well mate I'm sorry, I don't have any change on me right now. He grimaces at me when he hears my voice and sees that I'm wearing a dress.

"What?" I ask. Ila pulls on my arm, trying to move me along.

"Nothing." the man says, covering his face with his hat.

"I'm trans, you asshole. I'm glad I don't have anything to give you, if you're like that."

He doesn't say anything else, he just retracts into the darkness. I'm the worst person alive. I know.

"What the fuck is wrong with you?" asks Ila, quietly.

"He... he was being transphobic. You saw that, right?"

"No he wasn't."

"You know. He looked at me."

She stops holding my hand, then, and shoves both her fists deep into her coat's pocket.

We keep walking in silence. The moon is visible from the beach, but here we're too near the industrial estate to get a clear view of it. And the stars, well, they just aren't visible at all. The light pollution rises up to the clouds and turns the night sky into a dark orange chemical spill, and there's no sign that anything can live up there at all. I have put a piece of paper with an *X* on it in my back pocket, in the hopes that the energy of the room will be focused into this symbol, and will spend its time on that, rather than us. This is nonsense. I know it's nonsense, please stop telling me that it is, I have to try something, or else I am sure we won't survive the night. Trying to live only on the virtues of my stupid little rituals and sigils. Rituals completely unconnected to any sort of practise or craft, by the way. I just made them up in my head. But I check that the X is still there anyway, and it is. It helps me feel safer, even if it means nothing at all.

I wish this part, agonising as it is, stretched out forever. The long walk from Ila's flat to the House is the last moment where I am sure of everything. I can see Ila's breath in the air, I can feel her next to me, even if she doesn't hold my hand anymore. I can hear my feet on the paving slabs. There are baby foxes playing in the road.

I stop. "What if we just don't go?"

"God, don't do this now. We're nearly there."

"Why? Why can't we just turn around, and go back, and forget it and each other."

"You want to forget Hannah, too?"

That stops me.

"She's in there."

Really, Ila? Is she?

"I thought you didn't believe in that."

"Maybe not literally."

Ila is coming apart. I can tell. She believes so many things at once that her head is starting to hurt. She puts both of her hands on my shoulders and pleads, directly, to me.

"We can't turn back. I have to know, Alice. Please."

"And what if you find out something you don't want to?"

"Then my entire fucking life for the past three years will have been built on a lie. And I'll have to live with it. You should want this, you know. You might get to do what you all want to do, in the end."

"Which is?"

She kisses me. I can feel her tears on my cheeks, trying to freeze in the cold. Ila pulls away slightly but stays close.

"You get to prove a TERF wrong."

Ila once told me that horror should move on from relying on darkness as a symbol for the 'evil' or the unknown, because it advances racist thinking about blackness being evil and whiteness being good. I told her I thought that was stupid and we had an argument. I said that humans have always feared the dark and race has nothing to do with it, she said I was white, of course I'd say race had nothing to do with it, but race has everything to do with everything. Then we slept together, which has generally always been the pattern with us... argue, fuck, make up. Argue, fuck, make up. The arguing makes the fucking better. It fuelled it with a purpose. It felt like a game, each of us trying to win against the other, each of us vying to be on top.

The House is dark. Ila said we should bring a torch, but I told her that I couldn't cope with it. So we'll just have to feel our way through the darkness, hoping that we won't trip. It's dark, but as we stand there at the gate, our eyes adjust in a way they never did three years ago. The House wants us to look at it.

They tried to turn it into flats and failed. They tore away all the years of ivy which encased it, but, since it was abandoned again, the plants have regrown, creeping up its walls again like the repressed returning. The gates are still here, as they used to be, but the workmen must have torn down the old wall. In its stead there's construction fencing twisting around the House's perimeter. A cage. The House itself is still recognisable, but, if it was decaying before, now it has been fully cracked open. Beneath the ivy, much of its brickwork is gutted, open to the wind. Parts are wrapped in an old blue tarpaulin, and parts of that seem to have been snatched away by something.

Oh, what have they done to you? They tried to take you apart, didn't they? Did it hurt?

Yes.

The voice doesn't surprise me, really. It comes through the air into my skull like the words of an old friend. What did they do to you?

Men came and tried to turn me into something else with their tools and they tore at me until it hurt I bled all over them. I bled all over the earth. They didn't care at all they just kept ripping through my insides.

And then?

And then I took one in my hands. I drew him deep into me. He came into my heart and he saw how bright it was.

You made him do something, didn't you?

Yes.

Did he deserve it?

Yes.

What did you make him do?

The House doesn't answer me.

Ila pushes open part of the fencing, which isn't even properly secured.

"The construction stalled," she said, "because the site manager apparently went nuts. He attacked some of the other men working there, threw tools at them."

"That doesn't surprise me."

"Called them the n word. The official line was that he had a psychotic episode."

"Hmm."

Ila pushes through the gap she's made and holds it open for me to follow. It feels so much the same as it did three years ago, pushing through the artificial border. But it is also completely different. This time we have context. We know what we're in for, and we press onwards anyway, over the gulf. The grounds are thick with nettles and long grass. My hand is stung. I can feel the raised hive between my finger and thumb, and it stays there for five minutes before numbing. There is no longer a front door. The entrance is just an open maw now, a gaping hole which seems to swallow everything. The House might be allowing us to see it, but we can't see inside there. Maybe, just maybe, I should have let Ila bring a torch. But the thought of her holding it would have made me panic.

"Should we go in?" I ask.

"We know the way, right? I've replayed that night a hundred times in my head. We know the way."

I'm not so sure we do. Those corridors didn't make sense. We only navigated them because the House wanted us to.

But, I suppose, if the House wants us to get to the red room then we will get there. Ila grabs my hand and pulls me one last time into the dark.

We can see nothing at all at first. I can't even see Ila, although she's right in front of me, and I can even feel her hand firm on mine. The difference between having my eyes shut and open is nothing at all. I know where we are: standing in the entrance hall. I know that the dining room is off to one side, and the stairs are ahead. But whether any of these things are still intact is impossible to tell. The House could, for all I know, be entirely empty, with no floors left, just a great big cavernous void. A nothingness which surrounds us. Ila leads me forwards anyway. She is guiding me, but I get the horrible impression that something is guiding her in turn.

"The stairs are in front of us."

Her voice cuts through the emptiness and breaks it. When she speaks, suddenly, I can see, only dimly at first but then with more clarity. I can see the stairs, and I can see that almost all of them are collapsed in on themselves. The bannister that gave Hannah a splinter is gone completely. Above us I can see the sickening sky through the roof, which isn't there at all now. There are broken edges of it, and then nothing. All around us are parts of it, which, over time, have tumbled down and crashed, spreading broken tiles and brick and wood across the floor. Amongst all of this, I can see the corpses of birds and animals that must have wandered in through the unobstructed door and... been crushed by falling debris? I'm not sure. Some of them have been here for a while. Some of them seem so fresh that they could have died an hour ago. The smell of rot makes me want to gag. But through all of this there is a clear path, winding across the entrance hall and towards the stairs. And then, I can see, even as the stairs have collapsed, there are wooden planks laying up the length of them that someone could, if they were very careful, walk up. It would be hard to not fall. I guess they were put there during the attempt at construction work. Maybe. Or maybe you laid it out for us, House? A trail of breadcrumbs leading right to your oven.

I should leave. I should let go of Ila's hand and run back out into the real world. But I wouldn't be safe from it then, really. It has already been pushing into my life, through my walls, through my posters. Through my friends. Jon cutting his name into Sasha's body repeatedly. Jon and every man like him cutting every woman he knows up like collage with an old Playboy magazine until they are regurgitated, rearranged and neat. When he looked at me in that room at that party with those eyes. They were your eyes, weren't they, House? That was all you. You didn't make him do it, but he let you in. I know. I know you have always had me, and, if I run out of here, you'll always have me still. Ila and I... we never left this House. That's the truth of it. Sure, we stumbled out into the light of day, but enough of us stayed within, and enough of it stayed within us, that there was no real escape at all. So I let Ila pull me along, deeper and deeper into you. She steps, gingerly, onto the planks.

"You go up first," I say.

"Yeah, thanks. Very chivalrous."

There are enough of the steps on each side that it's possible to place one foot on there and the other on the hardwood plank. Ila's arms stretch out either side of her, swaying a little, like a tightrope walker. I go up after her, doing the same. It doesn't feel like you will let us fall. I do nearly trip at the last moment, but Ila holds me and stops me from tumbling back down the stairs. We're standing on the landing. I can see it all, now, in detail, despite how dark it must be. It's like we are in the middle of the daytime, although it must be close to midnight. And there they are, the doors. Doors, all along the length of the landing. I was worried this, too, might have rotted away, but it feels firm beneath me. All across it, obscuring the entrances to the doors, are more dead things. Badgers. Rats. Pigeons. Sprawled and still, limbs splayed out around them.

"What doorway is it?"

Ila walks towards one with a dead fox curled in front of it.

"This one."

"How do you know?" I ask, but I don't expect an answer, and one doesn't come.

We step over the fox. Its eyes are open, but they aren't there. Something has pecked at them and pulled them out. The corridor stretches down. I can see it. But apart from that, and the dead animals which scatter the length of it, it is the same as it always was. The same graffiti in the walls and on the floor. The same doors, positioned occasionally, always locked. Beneath our feet I spot the cadaver of a cat that has had its back cut open, and its spine pulled out. Some of the dead things are so old that they are just bones, or have become dried, mummified and unidentifiable shapes. And the smell. It grows stronger with every step. Ila's hold on my hand tightens.

I can hear something moving at the end of the corridor. We keep walking and turn at the junction to see a bird flapping. It's standing on the floor, and then it takes off into the air, but there is no room to move around. It just thumps into the wall and drops to the floor again. It's a crow. It looks at us and caws, loudly. I could swear that it sounds scared. It's just as anxious as we are. We walk towards it, and then when it's close it jumps up again. Ila nearly falls into me. She lets out a little scream that someday in the distant past, I would have teased her for. The crow flies up, and then loops further down the corridor, slamming into the ceiling, the wall, and the floor repeatedly. It's flying blind, I realise. We can see in the dark but the crow can't, the House has decided not to let it.

"We should follow it," Ila says, quietly, in my ear.

"Why?"

"Because it is being pulled to the same place as we are."

We turn the corner at the end of this hallway and see the crow sitting in the middle of the floor. It hops towards us, and peers at us curiously. Can it see now? Can it hear us?

There is a door at the end of the corridor, and it's open,

just slightly. Red light is seeping out through the crack, infecting the rest of the hallway. The bird turns from us and hops towards the door. It looks back again, as if to say, come on, I know why you're here, and then it flaps its wings into the room. Ila and I look at each other.

"I think we're supposed to follow," I say.

"That's the room." Ila looks scared now, far more so than I expected her to be.

"It's why we're here, right?"

"I know. But. Alice, I can feel it. I can hear it. Can you hear it, too?"

"Yes."

"What does it say?"

"It told me it hurt, when they tried to convert it. What does it say to you?"

Ila starts to walk backwards, away from me and away from the open doorway.

"I'm so sorry," she says, under her breath. "I'm so sorry, Alice."

"What does it say, Ila?" I don't let her run. I grab her and hold her in case she tries.

"It asked me to bring you here. And I did what it said. It wanted you, and it said it would let me go if I brought you here. Let go of me!"

She hits me in the face, and I spin away, into the nearest wall. There are words written deep into the fabric matter of the wall. *Welcome home Alice, Welcome home Ila, Welcome home.*

"It won't let you go!" I shout after her, and she stops. "Even if you try to leave. You know this corridor will just loop around back to the room, right? It wants us here."

"But it said..."

"And you believed it? After watching what it did to Hannah? You still did what it asked?"

Ila turns around to me.

"So what do we do?"

"We follow the crow. We go in, together. And we don't let it turn us against each other."

She laughs a cold laugh without humour. "And then what?"

"I don't know. But we're here. And the room is there, waiting for us. And you took us here, so you owe it to me now to come with me."

Ila sighs, deeper than she has ever sighed. She could still run. Run so far that the House vanishes into the distance. Move cities. She wanted to move city, after the first time she escaped. So did I. But we didn't. And if you asked either of us why we stayed here, we'd have no answer at all. I think that if we left, it would just have pulled us back again, though. She swallows and shuts her eyes tight, and when she opens them again she starts to walk forward. The light from the room is getting brighter. I know, in there I will find England's green and pleasant land, pasture, sick pasture, the festering cunt of this country, the flower of evil at its heart, when the Nazis won the war Winston Churchill hanged himself from the rafters of Downing Street rather than admit defeat, when he hanged himself his cock became erect (that happens when a body is hanged), and all the little children came in poked at his cock with sticks and laughed that the old fool was dead and gone. Fuck, I don't know what's happening to me. I'm broken, but I'm not alone, because she's here, and you're here, and Hannah lays ahead of me in the near distance, calling out voicelessly. We open the door, and the red light fills up our eyes, the brightest thing you've ever seen, sun in a village on an August day, flowers sprouting in the flowerbeds around the village green, the village they tore down the social housing for, the social housing over the road, torn down, to build this little idyllic blue heaven, God love us, God love us. They didn't tear down a village to build those flats. I need to think straight. I can't become irrational. I have to think straight and move forward, even as the door shuts behind us, and again, there's nothing on the other side but the end of the world. And in here, the red is vivid, and the lightbulb hangs like a star, and Hannah is nowhere to be seen. The bird that led us into the room has gone, it flew off into the English countryside I think.

HOUSE

The House spreads. Its arteries run throughout the country. Its lifeblood flows into Westminster, into Scotland Yard, into every village and every city. It flows into you, and into your mother. It keeps you alive. It makes you feel safe. Those same arteries tangle you up at night and make it hard for you to breathe. But come morning, you thank it for what it has done for you, and you sip from its golden cup, and kiss its perfect feet, and you know that all will be right in this godforsaken world as long as it is there to watch over you.

You, too, are implicated in its presence. Don't forget that. You, me. Those you love. The man who you watch walking his little dog along your road from your bedroom window. Your housemate and your lover and your Queen. Your MP and your favourite author. The shows you see on TV, and the films you see at the cinema. The streaming services and the producers of those streaming services and the city planners and the councils and the theatres and Banksy and the journalists and the people who pay them, the investors, the bankers, the internet users, the bitcoin miners, the electric car salesmen, the drones and the drone pilots and the video gamers who play as drones shooting at villages, the architects, the schoolboys, the poet laureate and the bricks that built the houses and the headmasters, the University Vice Chancellors, the church ministers, your grandparents, that band you like, so on and so on forever until I can't speak anymore, until my words become one long eternal howl.

In Italy, a huge painting named "The Apotheosis of Fascism" still stands. When Italy was making a bid for the 2024 Olympics in 2014, their Prime Minister stood in front of that very painting. It depicts Mussolini as a God. You can go to it, on your next holiday, and you can kneel down at its feet, and you can pray.

ILA AND ALICE

The room is as small and dull as it always was. And it is bright, brilliant, dazzling. On the far wall, where Hannah once hung, there is a brown stain. Alice recognises it. It's the same stain that waited beneath the poster in her room. From the ceiling, the lightbulb shines its light onto all the walls, and the walls shine their light back onto the girls, bathing them in their colour. The desk is still there. The floorboards are still bare beneath their feet. It is unchanged by the three years between the last time they saw it. It is exactly as it was in their nightmares. The stain that is Hannah spreads across the wallpaper opposite them, and as they step within the stain begins to coalesce into a clearer impression of Hannah's swastika shaped body. Alice can see it. Ila can see it. When Alice puts her ear to the wall, she can hear a high-pitched noise echoing within. Hannah is a blossoming flower of evil. Pluck it. Pluck it and give it to your darling lover. *Then, O my beauty! say to the worms who will devour you with kisses, that I have kept the form and the divine essence of my decomposed love!* The room contracts in. A noise fills the air, a whining, quiet at first but climbing in volume, louder until it becomes painful to hear. On the wall, the shape begins to move, darken. It gains clarity. The two girls press close together as they watch her push herself out of the vague other place beyond and into the room. The whine isn't a whine. It's a scream, and it comes from Hannah's open tortured mouth. Hannah is still screaming as she pushes herself free, through the wallpaper and into the world with them. They are nearly knocked down by the smell of her, the thick stench of years of shit and piss, which is smeared across her skin. When she moves, she moves with a wet, sticky sound. The last time they saw her, even twisted and broken, she still had perfect skin, somehow maintaining beauty and poise through the violence but... the three years have eaten at her. She is covered in her own filth, and her skin is as red as the wallpaper she crawled through. Her body is still bent into its crooked shape, but her hands are in motion, grasping, and finally she's free of the wall and falls onto the floor. Whatever held her strings has cut them. She shuffles forwards towards them, moving like a spider but every twitch of her limbs brings a grunt of pain. One of Hannah's limbs – it isn't clear if it is a foot or a hand, they are so distorted, reaches out to Ila, grasping at the air.

"We came back for you," says Ila.

She isn't sure if Hannah can even understand what she says. The girl's eyes, peering through a face riddled with aberrations, are clouded with a thick fog.

"Why?" she asks. Her voice is old. It sounds like it hasn't been used in years.

"Because we had to," Alice says.

"No, you didn't. No, no. God. You came back. You came back *here*." She lifts herself up, just slightly. With the movement, there comes a cacophony of tiny cracks from inside her. Her hair was once so gorgeous, but now it is slick with filth, stuck in strands to her skull. "You can't get me out of here. I gave myself to him, completely."

Ila bends down towards her, and offers a hand to her face, gently cradling it. Her skin feels like paper beneath her fingertips.

"Who did you give yourself to?" She talks to Hannah like she is talking to a small child, or an animal who is ill.

"Don't talk down to me you bitch."

She tries to shove Ila off of her, but it only succeeds in seeming pathetic. Her limbs, bent and fused, have lost all strength. But she had enough bile within her to growl at Ila.

"I worshipped at his alter," she spat, "I supplicated myself to Albion, and I wished for a day that he would rise from the ground and stand over this land. I did that, and I watched you hurt one another, and I knew what I had done was terrible, but you came back, you came back, you came back."

Alice hears it. A click. She looks up, away from her friends, and sees the second door. It has been there in the corner of the room, always shut. Always locked. But she looks and realises the door handle is turning. Something on the other side is opening it.

"Ila," says Alice, but she doesn't hear. She's listening to Hannah's bubbling, angry words.

The door begins to swing inwards, slowly. The crack widens. On the other side... Alice is entranced. There is no shape opening up the door, nobody on the other side.

"Come close," whispers Hannah. "Come close. You make me sick. You want to leave?"

"Yes," says Ila.

"Then come close. Lean down to me and let me speak how."

And the broken thing that used to be Hannah tells Ila what to do. But Alice doesn't listen. She stands, nervously, and looks through the newly opened door. Through it, she sees something, a colossal body wreathed in sunlight. And as she watches, it begins to dance.

YOU

And did those feet in ancient times... did they? Well? I have
yet to be given an answer. I am in the dark, asleep, perhaps. I
have not woken up for I cannot see the sun. I have not woken
up now. I cannot see my son, they have put him into a flat box
and thrown it from the roof with great and utter joy. I jumped
after him, or tried to, but they pulled me back. The woman –
its mother – the child's mother – jumped after the child, falling
to her death onto the cobblestones, a bloody pulped mess of a
woman. Call the cops on this worship, they are trying to build
Jerusalem in England's green and pleasant land, not trying to
build England's green and pleasant land in Jerusalem, which
is the correct way of going about things – nothing so green
nothing so pleasant about the work that sets us free – but no
matter – the world is one great house with England at the
heart of it, as the master bedroom perhaps or, no, the master's
study, the master's tools made in the master's study by the
master, well actually the master thinks up the ideas and gets
the women out clawing at the walls to create the master's

tools and they cannot dismantle the master's house genuinely as they are made from the same materials as the master's house, so when you try to take a bit off the master's house, the tool just replaces that bit, on and on like that you see? Some see nature all ridicule and deformity! Some scarce see nature at all! I can't see nature at all! All I see is things to build or use to build! But don't forget that England's green and pleasant land is and always will be holy land, better land, strange land, both God's own country and a godless place, where the earth-mother still dwells and pulls herself up from deep under the thick green moss showing off her white skin showing off her fertile body don't you want to fuck her hard God reaching down from the heavens, his prick firm and hard, entering into Mother Earth's tight wet cunt, and that is England born from that coupling don't you see, witches burning black suns into the sky, and a virgin hanged from the great oak in the middle of the forest glade. Beneath your feet Albion lays. Further down, further than anyone would ever dig. He lays, and he dreams of rising, but he doesn't. It stops him.

It sits under a tree, the same tree the virgin dangles from, birds pecking at her now, she's been there long enough, it sits underneath her looking up her skirt admiring the view. It sits from a high ivory tower admiring the view. It sits building things, knocking them down like little games. It sits and waits. It gets up it walks down at night with its friends to smash in the windows of fags and synagogues and fag synagogues and Jew fag bars, and breaks up the headstones of AIDS victims in the cemetery with the worker's hammers, with the master's tools. Dead Churchill, pulled down from the place his corpse hangs, and mutilated, circumcised. Unstitched. Like an older sweater pulled until he came undone, and you laugh at him, because it's funny, because it's funny to see the old cunt dead and gone.

There was a little boy being circumcised. They slipped, they cut the little baby boy's penis open into a flower and in the emergency room turned it into a little vagina, and the little boy grew up never knowing, but he wanted to be a boy, see, and however many times he pleaded to G-d that he should wake up the next day as a boy G-d did not answer, and that is how you know that we are either holy or unholy, either a part of the grand design of the universe or a flaw or a symptom of perfection elsewhere. They studied the boy. Like an experiment. And he hated them for it, and he hated himself for it.

Jacob is a fifteen-year-old boy who dreams that he is a girl. Every night he wonders what it is like to be a girl. His girlfriend dresses him up in one of her dresses, puts make up on, and crawls underneath his skirt to suck him off. He dreams that it could be like this. She tells him it is fine if this is just a fetish but he might seriously have a problem actually, so he tells his mother, mother sometimes I wish I was born a girl, and his mother beats him half to death with a frying pan. He dreams his name is Alice and he is in his twenties and he is a rape victim stuck in the innermost room of a haunted house screaming whilst his best friend and rapist stands with him screaming too, and beneath their feet a girl who is a symbol lays and she dies then, finally free, and the room pulses and stretches as tall as the sky and they stand within the redness of it screaming and sobbing and holding one another. Jacob dreams this. He watches in the dream as one girl tries her best to stop being who she is, while the other tries to be who she is. One girl breaks her nose like an egg, bleaches her skin until it shines, then she bends down and takes the other girl's cock in her hand and tries to cut away, tries to open it up into a flower, and Jacob doesn't want to watch any more, and one girl is saying to the other don't you want to die as a girl?

We don't need to dream that the Nazis won world war two, the fascists are already here, on our streets, every day, can't you see them? They're the man next to you in the shop. The woman smoking outside the pub. They're all around us. They're in the government. They won.

Don't you want to die as a girl?

Jacob doesn't know why he dreams this. He creates a profile on a website under the name Alice, and pretends to be a twenty-six-year-old woman. He draws himself roughly as Alice, and he thinks he looks so much better there, and he would be so much happier if he was a twenty-six-year-old woman. His mother finds the picture and beats him again, sends him off to therapy. He doesn't want to be a woman anymore.

The world Jacob lives in is much like yours. It has the same buildings and the same fields and the same men and the same woman but only men and women. When Jacob is eighteen he meets two other girls – a brown girl called Ila, and a young woman named Hannah. Hannah becomes his best friend and eventual wife. Ila is eventually vanished, I don't know where. They send her back to her own country. She was born in the UK but they still send her back. Jacob and Hannah have lots of little babies, lots of little babies running free. We have to secure a future for our children, he tells himself. We have to secure a future for our children and our land. We have to secure a future for our children and our green and pleasant land, our Jerusalem, a picture of Powell on the wall of every classroom in England, yearly competitions to see who will get to read *rivers of blood* on Radio 4 this year, which is the highest of honours that can be bestowed to man (or woman! Let's not be sexist here). A Northern comedian jokes about 'pudding of colour' because he 'doesn't know if it's politically correct to say black'. I don't know what he means by that, I don't know what he says, but maybe he could identify as an attack helicopter, and maybe I identify as an attack helicopter over Iraq shooting down hellfire on villagers and little children; maybe that's just *my* gender and you have to look at it and say yes however much it scares the living daylights out of you, because if you don't I will firebomb your home, I will take your grandmother on a helicopter ride up to the top of the sky and drop her out like I'm Pinochet like this is Chile welcome to hell bitch welcome to this death flight you old bitch – *heavy breathing, there is heavy breathing and the speaker struggles to say whatever they wanted to say next as they are overcome with passionate emotion and hatred towards your grandmother. It's six o'clock. Do you know where your grandmother is?*

My grandmother owned a glassware factory in pre-revolutionary Cuba, my grandmother was a member of a death squad, my grandmother killed your grandmother at least by the virtue of not trying to stop your Grandmother from dying or being killed, dropped into the water from a great, great height, dropped down from the top of a tower to fertilise the green and pleasant land.

Jacob reaches twenty-six years of age. He's married with children. Ila is somewhere else, not here. Hannah stands at Jacob's side, hugging him and kissing his neck softly. But one night, she walks into their bedroom, and he thought she was busy outside, see, she sees that he is dressed in her lingerie, wearing her makeup on his face, applied badly, he's twenty-six when this happens remember, they both are. She sees this, and he screams at her, please, please, don't tell anybody, please, you are my loving wife I *order* you not to tell anybody. But she calls the police. She says, my husband has been dressing up in my clothes, wearing my make up, I think he is a gay fag, she says. She's scared, because if she now knows, others could know... he could be out fucking men in the bushes in the countryside, and people would think she is allowing this, and she'd end up going down with him. She doesn't have time to think about whether she actually thinks it's okay and that he can dress how he wants. She calls the police. My husband is a gay fag. He wears my stockings. Before she can finish the call, she's crying, into the phone I mean, and before she can finish making the call, Jacob grabs a claw-hammer from the cupboard, walks through the house, into the kitchen where Hannah is on the phone, and smashes the hammer into the back of her head. She drops to the floor, and the phone hangs from its wire, swaying slightly. Hannah is on the floor twitching involuntarily. Jacob drops the hammer. What has he done... what he has done. He can't believe it. She's still alive, but only just. Her arms flail out towards him, so he goes to the knife rack. He takes the sharpest blade there is. He bends over her and brushes the hair from her eyes and coos at her that he loves her, that's he's sorry. But he isn't a fag. He holds the blade tip to the skin on her arm. *I am not a fag.* Property of Jacob. Property of Jon. Every man who has ever hurt a woman crumples into his head, only to find that they don't fit in here at all. It's all wrong in here. The Society for Cutting Up Women leaves, grumbling about how it isn't how it used to be.

He hangs himself from the light fixture, using the tie he wore to their wedding. The police find them there. His body is still wearing Hannah's underclothes. His kids are still asleep upstairs. My Mummy killed my Mummy, my Daddy killed my Mummy, my, my, Hannah's red lipstick is smeared across his face. They arrest his body and put it on trial for being a gay fag, and also, they suppose, for being a murderer, which is second to being a gay fag really, most gay fags are also murderers. Once you have broken one social norm, well, what comes next really, oh, what comes next... if Jacob survives then Jacob is forcibly sterilised, cut open and turned inside out right, the smell's fucking awful maybe the eventuality where he dies is better, because now he's a hollow shell of a woman walking down a polluted riverbank, drinking in the dark fumes of the satanic mills and wishing that he had killed his wife and then himself, and wishing that he was in a red room in the heart of a nameless city in England. Because now I am alone and when I wake up tomorrow maybe something will have gone wrong and here I am, inside this world. Here I am. My name is Jacob or Alice and I am pulled out of my house by masked men and kept inside a box until then they pull me out. They say, wear a dress. I don't want to wear a dress. I only wear dresses when I feel comfortable wearing dresses. I do not feel comfortable right now. But no matter. I have to wear the dress. And then I am here, on the floor, with all Ila standing over me dressed in latex. Ila standing over me in black latex. Ila She Wolf of the SS stands over me kicks me in the stomach I scrabble at her but she knows she's won. They didn't vanish her, she assimilated, she became part of the system just to survive, you understand, she had to do this to survive. She reaches down her latex skirt and pulls out her bloody tampon and shoves it into my mouth and I choke but I do not choke to death and Albion watches and Ila is so worried because he knows he might be next, they might work out how it feels when he dreams of a world where he is a boy called Jacob or Xander or Harry, she thinks he thinks maybe Albion can see inside, Albion says, yes, kill this shitty pig, and all the people watching at home, all the wives cooking dinner, the husbands home from work, the little kids home from school squealing in delight. And the wives cooking dinner are emancipated. The producers of the show are the BBC. They ask commentators to discuss the events happening to the shitty transvestite pigs. Those commentators are generally feminists who self-describe as gender critical and often appear on Newsnight or Women's Hour, and this happens *God* is a self-described feminist and so are the latex babes so is Ila queen of the latex babes she-wolf and so am I. So are all shitty transvestite pigs. Now do you see? Sigmund Freud was killed years ago as a shitty transvestite pig. In front of living cameras, in front of a live audience, they say, don't you have the self-control to not be like this, don't you have the self-control to either be a woman or man, not to be this transvestite pig, this it, this it-pronounced pig, pig with *it*-pronouns, they throw me into a garbage truck, amongst all humanity's shit, I am screaming, God is laughing, all my friends are laughing, some touch themselves, am I a girl? Am I just a shitty pig? Sick the union now down to the bottom of your own building the great open wide sky, the skylight, the top of the building, the ledge, I'm on a ledge, I felt. I feel somebody opening up to me. I think I heard somebody opening up to me. No you can't. No you can't. I will take you home. Open up. Open up. Open up. The door in the corner of the room which has always been locked opens up and what comes out... No. This computer terminal has become infected with a disease, it is swelled, it is all wrong, can't you see, can't you see, the computer's flesh has swelled it is filled with pus, it is seeping disgusting pus. The pus is dripping down the computer into a bowl. Every five hours a man enters the room. His face is not visible. He enters the room wearing a boiler suit and he removes the bowl, filled with pus, and replaces it with an empty bowl. He takes the bowl away. We do not see where.

You have no identity. When you are stopped by the pigs they ask for your ID but you have to say you are not a person, you are a pig like them, you are a shitty pig, I will slaughter you round the neck with a knife or a bolt in your shitty pig brain, squeal!!!!!!!!!!!! Squeal! oink oink baby. Baby. Fucking r_____ baby. Fucking baby with no brain you stupid slutty r_____ tranny baby. I will take everything you have. On the computer screen is the Latex Babe TV Show. This is your favourite TV show. It is on TV every night and you watch it every night. You have to. You sing the theme song in your sleep. I felt ashamed but I didn't do anything. You talk to your union and vote for a small snail shell as the new boss. You vote for a tiny baby rabbit as the boss. But Ila comes from the dark and takes your union leader and he is now the guest on the Latex Babe TV Show, he is a little snail, he is a tiny little rabbit, the Ila crushes your Union Leader with her heels. This building. This grey building. Disappeared inside yourself, disappeared by her own discomfort, called a r_____ by a woman wearing a latex dress, that's not an ok word to say, that's not an ok word to say, not hers to reclaim, I wasn't saying it to reclaim it, she says, I was saying it to hurt you, it is a word meant to hurt, does your cum have blood in it? Are you a tiny pig hanging from the slaughterhouse ceiling of outsourced work? Crushing device. By the colour of smog I open up your house, I am in your house, I am being tortured on your diseased computer screen, with no religious recourse, with no safety net, the nanny state has bad teeth that are all inside out, they are fleshy, they hurt, long live the new state, long live the new flesh and drink this dry, drink this dry, am I girl, am I just a pig?, am I a girl, am I just a pig?, am I a shitty girl, am I just a shitty pig?, will I be thrown out with the garbage like all the other pigs?, anti-socialist press flat against the metal crushing device, now don't tell me you want to repent your shitty pig ways now, now don't tell me: you don't like this dream and you would like another? Jacob by the Thames thinks this. Alice in the room thinks this. Ila in the room thinks this. England thinks this. England is the only place. England eats every other place. England eats people, too. Look at the Thames, choked with the bodies of migrant workers pushed in there by drunken Prime Ministers, and the Prime Minister fucking sex workers who he has asked to say oh aren't you a bad boy aren't you, aren't you a bad boy. There is a poem by the late Sean Bonney which goes like this:

"So anyway, I killed Boris Johnson.

You know who he is, yeh?

Not much of a crime, really.

It was, I dunno, 2005, maybe 2006

he was on his bike

going down the Charing Cross Road

and me, I was on foot, of course.

Anyway, there was a bus behind him

and I took my chance. I pushed him under

the bus went over and then he was dead.

Noone saw me. Noone stopped me.

Everything that's happened since has been

a dream. A deep and horrible dream.

Wake up. For the sake of us all, wake up."

I have to believe that was reality. I have to believe that *is* reality, and that this world is just a parody, a parody, a red room, a metaphor for a worse world. I keep trying to wake up but I can't. My friends are all breaking their faces, committing grievous self-harm just for the chance to live. I say 'my friends' – I'm doing that, too. I'm cutting myself up. I feel like any real woman knows how to do this, to completely unstitch herself to reveal the true form, a form that the entity in the room will be satisfied with. Many women are doing this! Women from all over England are pulling themselves apart and crawling, like new, wet, bloody, sickly babies, screaming for milk, crawling out from their old husks of bodies, into the new day. Luckily many do this over breakfast, and milk is easy to come by at breakfast, because everybody in England drinks milk with their breakfast food, in tea or coffee or just a nice refreshing glass of white pure milk for baby. I know women who have done this. And their new forms are so beautiful, so raw and genuine and honest and brave, new forms which are able to get books published, or get opinion pieces in various newspapers. These new forms log onto Twitter and get effortlessly popular on there. I know this to be true. And I sometimes think that what I want is really misogynistic. Sometimes in the worst moments I ask if the TERFs are right and me wanting a cunt and tits and nice hair is because I'm a self-centred male monster and I want to be in bathrooms and changing rooms and I want to win women's sports competitions and laugh because they can't say anything and I want to win the Women's Fiction Prize and they'll say but look that's not a woman and the thought police will come for them for thinking that but in actual fact they'll probably just get an OBE for it and get a book deal and then what will I be? I want to be a woman. I am a woman. I want a cunt because lots of women have cunts. It is not violent to myself or to others. It is a good thing. It is a positive for the world to have more women, with or without cunts. I remember a story I read once, that said real women all do this, they all pull themselves apart, they all have real selves beneath, so I try to do the same. Ila tries to watch, but I make her turn around to look at the wall. I can't stop Hannah from looking at me of course... but is she even a person these days, no, she might not be a person. I try to do it, I pull at my belly button, I find a nerve ending which comes undone, I unravel and scream in pain as blood begins to burst out of me and splatter over the floor. I slip on my own blood and fall down onto my back, still pulling myself apart for the art, screaming, hey look at me, I can do this too, I can be like you strong brave clever honest women, look! Look! *Look!* And Ila turns around and sees that I have disemboweled myself. *Oh baby*, she says, *no baby no, that isn't how this is done. You can't do this. This knowledge is available to women and women alone, and you are not a woman, you wish you were but you aren't, so in trying to reveal your true form you have simply mutilated yourself horribly, and now you are going to bleed to death. You poor thing. You poor delusional man.*

Ila's new true form has a nose which is unbroken, a little cute button nose, and she has bleached her skin. She is utterly false and utterly honest. The room is happy with her, and it will release her, out onto the streets. Her skin sears with immense pain from the bleach. It bubbles, it burns, it scars, she will never be the same again. She will never be happy. But she will have survived fascism, which is something, surely, she will have lived.

Alice is entirely undone, but she tries to lift herself up, her insides sliding out around her. *Look at me*, she says. *This is the most honest I have ever been with anybody. This. My body. My insides. I'm bearing it all. I did this for you, Ila. Not for Hannah. I don't care about Hannah anymore. She was a victim of this ideology that corrodes our lives. I'm talking about me and you, Ila, you and I, we were best friends, we loved each other, and now we hate each other, and I did this because I do still care about you, because I want you to like me. Look at me!* Alice is crying, trying to hold in all of her internal organs in her arms. Ila is crying too. *But*, Ila says, *but why. I don't want this! I don't want you to hurt yourself! I always told you, don't get the operation Alice! You'll regret it!* Alice laughs, *oh this isn't like that operation, though, this isn't a vaginoplasty, it's what you think a vaginoplasty is, it's what you wish it was actually*. Ila cries harder because Alice is right. She wanted this. Vaginoplasty is a safe procedure, it is not anything like self-mutilation. And Alice cries looking at Ila, skin peeling away, nose all wrong, because she wanted that, too. They wanted the best for each other, or thought they did. And look where it has gotten them. They're so focused on each other that Hannah has gone, turned to dust, and maybe she was never there in the first place, maybe she just died from a drug overdose and they buried her out in the forest behind the house and nobody ever thought that was a possibility. Alice, guts trailing across the floor, shuffles towards her friend. They embrace, covered in each other's insides. *I love you*, says Ila. *I love you*, says Alice. And the world comes crashing down around them. Maybe they'll be okay. Do you think they'll be okay, in the end? I think they will be. I have to think they will be.

ALICE AND ILA

Ila and Alice both make it out of the House alive. They stumble back down the street and into Ila's bed, crying together well into the next day. Ila's skin is not bleached, although her nose is a little bruised. Alice has not been cut open. They don't sleep together.

The following week, Alice moves out of her flat and into Ila's. It feels like the most natural thing in the world to do – they love each other, despite everything, and they will continue to love each other until the end of time.

A month or so later, both girls go back to the House. They pour lighter fluid around the circumference of it, in a great, wide ring. Alice sets it alight. The old ivy burns well, but they stand well back because the smoke that billows out from it is toxic. The ivy catches alight, then the House itself, or what remains of it, goes up in flames.

"It's so beautiful," says Alice, and hugs Ila to her closely. They stand there as long as they dare. The fire spreads out, and, in the centre, it folds around the red room, the walls melt away until there is only a pure colourless centre. Then, even that is gone. The people in the block of flats over the street stand at their windows watching it in amazement, and by the time the fire brigade show up, both girls are gone, and the House is as good as gone too. Just black ash drifting in the night air.

EPILOGUE

GLAD DAY

It takes time, but eventually a contractor buys the land and begins to build on the ground where there was once a very evil House. People tell the men working there, hey, this used to be a haunted house, but the men laugh, because they don't believe in ghosts. They're rational men. A new block of flats goes up. Families move in. In a flat on the third floor, a family lives, and they have a son. And that son is confused and lonely. His parents are panicked, manic things.

The face in his wall is ignored. It screams, banging its fists against the inside of the building, but he can't hear. He sits on his computer, looking at the forums, and the pdf files people send him. There is a storm coming, say the men online.

The boy begins to learn things. He begins to learn about chemistry, and the chemical compounds to create an explosion. It's not too hard, really. He realised that he had most of the things he needed at home, and the rest he managed to steal from school. His parents didn't know at all. The government didn't know, either. They didn't think to look at him. Why would they?

I'm going to do it, he tells the men online, anonymously. Someone posts something like this every day. They're always posting that they're going to do it, they're going to go after that girl that rejected them, they're going to bring a gun to school, and so on and so on. This happens enough times that the people on the forum don't really believe anyone now. But the boy posts it anyway. Sure, the people say. Do it. Go on.

He makes the bomb. He makes a mechanism that will ignite it if he calls a burner phone he straps to it, and he puts it in his rucksack. He is quiet and clever and resourceful. He knows that the Pride parade is coming up next week. It is the height of summer, and his room is a cube of sweat. Hannah, in the wall, watches helplessly as he picks up his bag on the day of the parade and leaves. A glad day will come, he thinks. A glad day will dawn.

It is, almost, like it used to be. They push into the parade, in the middle of the crowd, and the security guards come for them but they can't do anything.

"Fuck," says Harry sweat dripping from his hairline. "I've missed this."

Alice marches next to him. She's holding a loudspeaker in one hand and is getting ready to shout into it with all the force she has in her lungs. But before she does, she looks down at Harry. She's so much taller than him. It's almost comical, but at the same time people find it sweet, their height difference. Harry feels like he's gotten shorter since he started taking T, which is probably just a trick of his mind, but it pisses him off anyway.

Their fingers are entwined. Alice holds the loudspeaker to her mouth. "The government," she calls into it, and her voice expands up and down the street, "are trying to bring back Section 28! They are trying to make it illegal to discuss transness in public! That is the endgame here! What do we say to that?"

Everyone else in the crowd, Harry included, responds. "Fuck off!"

"That's right!" shouts Alice. "What was the first pride, everyone?"

"A riot!" they call back.

"What was that?"

"A riot!"

The people watching from the side-lines of the parade, who came here to see pink things and floats and a particular kind of gayness, are nervous. One of them, a man, calls out at them. "Stop ruining it!" he shouts. But they march onward.

Harry loves Alice more than he thought it was possible to love another human, and he loves her, seeing her there, striding like a giant, holding the loudspeaker like a sword. He scratches his face, and feels the beard that has grown there bountifully since he started T. He worries that it doesn't look enough like a real beard, but whenever he vocalises this Alice kisses his cheeks and tells him he is beautiful, and he kisses her back and says, darling you're so handsome. Harry can't believe he used to hate her. He can't believe he would have once been a counter protestor, screaming that the group of trans people who had pushed their way into pride were a bunch of misogynists. Sometimes, the old version of himself floats above him near his bedroom ceiling, and tells him he'll always be Ila, but that happens less and less now. Ila isn't a real person, these days. That was another person, in another time.

They are still marching along the street. The sides of the road are lined with people, bus stops, benches. And under one of those benches, the boy, who stands close but not too close, has stuffed his rucksack. He watches, waiting.

Them

says a voice. It doesn't scare him. It feels comforting, like the words of a loving parent, but it makes him feel far safer than either of his parents' voices made him feel.

That group there you see them don't you how do they make you feel?

They make me feel angry, he thought.

Why do they make you feel angry?

They are hedonists, they are degenerates, they are part of the plague that tears this country down into the dirt.

This is a parade full of people like that but you hate them more don't you why do you hate them more?

Because they scream.

Yes.

They scream hysterically. It hurts my head. It hurts my ears.

They scream like Heidegger as a woman yes so do it then

says the voice

do it then come home, come home.

They march up the street, and he watches them as just another random onlooker. They get closer. Their voices grow louder. The tall tranny with the loudspeaker is shouting nonsense to the sky. He waits, until the group is in line with the bench, and then he calls the number. His heart is thumping. What if it doesn't work? He might have fucked up the whole thing. What if it doesn't work, and he's just another liar posting on the forum, claiming he's going to be the one to do it when in reality he's too much of a fucking idiot to do anything at all. But then it comes. The elation. The euphoric burst of light that shoots through him, golden, and he feels like he could fly as the bomb goes off, shooting parts of the bench high above everyone's heads. The force of the explosion knocks everyone down, even him. He thought he was standing far enough away, but no, he falls, into the pile of degenerates around him, crushed beneath their bodies, spluttering for air. He pushes through them and pulls himself up into his brave new world, above his lessers who are still crawling in the dirt beneath him. He can see them, the group. They were knocked down, and parts of the bench smashed into them. They are scattered around, bodies over bodies, blood pooling underneath them. He looks down upon them and knows that he will be a legend. Soon there will be sirens. He leaves before they can get to him, but they will. They'll come to his flat, and pull him from his room, the eyes in the wall oozing tears. The policemen will arrest him, peacefully. Maybe they will take him to McDonald's first, before they go to the station.

As he eats his burger, the policeman will look at him and ask, oh son, why did you do this? And the boy will take another bite. I have to believe my life has meaning, he thinks. I have to believe that I have worth.

But for now he leaves, as if he was never there. Amongst the rubble, Harry lies, feeling the dead weight of others on top of him. He splutters. There's no sound at all. He wonders why it's silent, before realising that the explosion has destroyed his hearing. There are limbs all around him. Most of them are connected to bodies. Most of them are moving. Some are not. He crawls through the bodies, and the rubble. The sunlight feels brighter than it did before. Alice is lying close to him, her eyes open. At first he panics, but then her head turns towards him. She mouths something, but he can't hear. She mouths it again, and he understands. He goes to her, on his hands and knees, rubble and blood and bodies all around them. The police, the ambulance, the news crews. They are coming. Photographers are taking pictures of them, and they will put these pictures on the front pages of newspapers, and the picture will be with them forever, they won't ever escape it, two trans people covered in blood and embracing amidst the carnage. The photographer who gets the image wins a prize for it. They don't know that yet. They only know this: Harry crawls towards Alice with the last of his strength, his arms outstretched and reaching. The rain will come. When it does it will be bloody. The future will be red-tinted and unknowable, but they will be together. Come to me now, mouths Alice. Hold me.

ACKNOWLEDGEMENTS

Jenn and Ellis from Cipher have provided me with a valuable platform that I never expected to get. It feels so surreal to me every day that this book is a thing. Thank you so, so much, for taking a chance on an extremely wild and gross book that I was certain was unpublishable. And thank you to Wolf and to Wolf's wife, too, for the brilliant cover.

During the initial drafting process, some people were kind enough to read this book. Mimi, Emily Bergslien and Kat Weaver, Constance Savage, Francine Toon, Harry Josephine Giles: thank you all so much, without your helpful comments and feedback I would probably have given up on it.

Thank you to Kat Sinclair, Nehaal Bajwa and James Garwood Cole, for your nights and days of friendship. May we chill out together again soon.

I started writing this book at the urging of Jess Burgess, and read them the opening in their living room whilst drinking hot tea that they brought to me. They said they liked it. They later read a first draft and cried at the ending, which made me feel powerful.

Julia Armfield and Rosalie Bower thank you for keeping

my head from melting, and for hyping this book up. Thank you to Eliza Clark in this regard as well.

Christie – *Princess Prosecco* is going to fuck the world up.

This novel is indebted to the grand tradition of queer horror, from Shirley Jackson and Daphne Du Maurier to Helen Oyeyemi and Clive Barker. There are more writers that I love than I can name here, but their work is folded into every sentence of what I write.

Tell Me I'm Worthless was written in the haze of the first lockdown, after I retreated from the very small room I rented in someone else's house back to my parents' place. So firstly I have to thank them, for providing me with a place to hide from the world for a little while, and for forcing me to go outside and touch grass every couple of days. But they probably shouldn't be reading this, considering they aren't meant to be reading the book due to all the sex, so they'll never know I thanked them here. So it goes.

In the summer of 2021 I met and fell in love with Oleander Gravett. The text of these acknowledgements was already set back then for the initial UK publication, and it would have been a little strange to mention her given we'd only just found one another. However, I'd like to thank her here for welcoming me into her life and for enriching it in every way.

I'd also like to thank Kristin Temple and the team at Nightfire who worked on the US publication of this book for being surprisingly receptive to not changing references to British things, and for putting together such a cool cover, and for publishing me alongside so many wonderful books.

ABOUT THE AUTHOR

ALISON RUMFITT is a writer and semiprofessional trans woman. Her debut pamphlet of poetry, *The T(y)ranny*, was a critical deconstruction of Margaret Atwood's work through the lens of a trans woman navigating her own misogynistic dystopia. Her work has appeared in countless publications, such as *Sporazine, Datableed, Bloody Women, Burning House Press, Soft Cartel, Glass: A Journal of Poetry*, and more. Her poetry was nominated for the Rhysling Award in 2018. You can find her on Twitter @hangsawoman and on Instagram at alison.zone. She loves her friends. *Tell Me I'm Worthless* is her debut novel.